"The story of our marriage is all over the neighborhood."

Harry draped his arm over Stacey's shoulder. "So I thought, if you have no objection, I might call on you from time to time for a little more bridal work."

"Sort of like rent-a-bride?" Stacey suggested lightly. But the tinkling laugh she forced out to show him how casual she was about the idea sent a chill down her spine.

"Sort of," Harry agreed. "I've got a million things to do, now that everything is under control here. I'll keep you posted. And you keep my telephone number close by, in case you need a husband again."

Long after he'd gone, Stacey sat, idly twirling the wedding rings she had never got around to removing. *It had been so pleasant being Mrs. Harry Marsden.*

EMMA GOLDRICK

rent-a-bride ltd

Harlequin Books

TORONTO • NEW YORK • LONDON
AMSTERDAM • PARIS • SYDNEY • HAMBURG
STOCKHOLM • ATHENS • TOKYO • MILAN

Harlequin Presents first edition December 1985
Second printing January 1986
ISBN 0-373-10841-9

Original hardcover edition published in 1985
by Mills & Boon Limited

CHAPTER ONE

SHE started shivering just as the airplane banked and turned out over the calm surface of Lake Waco, to the west of the central Texas city of the same name. She wrapped her arms around herself to keep control, but it was difficult. Her eighteenth birthday had passed without celebration or comment, and the quick trip to the law offices in Dallas had left her more confused than before. Aunt Ellen had prodded and poked at her without mercy, until finally Stacey had signed all the papers without reading any of them, just to find a little peace.

'Now all that's settled,' her aunt had said, 'we can get back to the ranch. George will be waiting for you.' She spoke in a nasal simper. The sound irritated Stacey as much as the words did. Yes, of course, her dulled brain snarled at her, George will be waiting for you. And so will Uncle Henry. And of the two, her uncle was the one she feared most. Dear Uncle Henry, who had come down the pike with hardly a shirt to his back, and married Aunt Ellen for the money she didn't possess! As soon as he had found out that it was all Stacey's money, that was when son George had popped up.

'He'll make a fine husband for you,' Aunt Ellen kept insisting. 'And it will knit the family together. Won't that be lovely?' Of course, Stacey muttered under her breath. Lovely for George, or for Aunt Ellen? Poor Aunt Ellen, whose face was disfigured by a huge strawberry birthmark on her left cheek. And who seemed to fear her husband more than she loved him.

Poor Aunt Ellen, who, in all the confusion, had come to the Dallas airport, only to find that the power of attorney she wanted was still in their hotel room. So, somehow or another, Stacey found herself boarding the plane alone. Making her first adventure outside the boundary of Rancho Miraflores since her—what?— fourteenth birthday. But of course Uncle Henry would be waiting for her at the terminal in Waco. 'And here, take your pills while I'm watching,' her aunt ordered.

Stacey swallowed them down without protest. Her pills were no longer something she fought over. They had just seemed to appear, without a doctor's visit, two years before. Well, she kept telling herself, they *did* reduce her tensions, relax her. In fact, they usuallly put her to sleep. Except at times like this when she was violently excited.

The touch of a hand on hers snapped her back to reality. The young man in the adjoining seat was trying to prise her clenched fingers loose from the arm that separated them. 'It's a perfectly normal landing,' he assured her. 'Relax! Is this your first flight?'

Her eyes moved slowly down to where his right hand clasped her left. His thumb smoothed the skin on the back of her hand, gently, warmly. Almost in a daze her eyes wandered up to his face. He topped her five foot seven by a good head, she noted. Wide-set dark eyes, under a fringe of curly brown hair. Craggy. Not hand-some, just—vibrant.

'Lord help us, you'll shake yourself to death, girl!' With one easy motion he flipped up the separating arm and pulled her close up against him. For a micro-second she struggled, her innate anger driving, but then a combination of events took over. She recalled the last time she had been enfolded in strong loving arms. When she was thirteen, and her father had hugged her tight and then gone off to Vietnam—and never returned. Her muscles relaxed as she savoured the warm comfort. She leaned her head over against his chest, and the steady rhythm of his heart comforted. One of his hands tangled in her hair and gently stroked her into a hypnotic state. The wheels of the aircraft touched ground, squealed, and began to run true as the nosewheel made contact.

'There now, everything's home safe.' He pushed her slightly away, but still in the circle of his arms.

'I wasn't afraid of the plane,' Stacey half whispered, staring at him. Look! She commanded her hazy mind. Look at him! The corners of his mouth seemed perpetually turned up into a grin. He's got a strong nose—a Roman nose. What is he? A displaced centurion? Why am I wandering like this? She snatched her eyes away from him and looked out the window.

The plane had taxied off the runway on to the concrete apron in front of the terminal, and a couple of baggage handlers came out of the building and headed for the parking area. The high-winged twin engine commuter plane trundled up to the same area, swung around in a half-circle, and stopped. The motors roared once, muttered to a stop, and coughed. The tri-blade propeller just outside Stacey's window twirled for a time or two, then it too came to a stop.

There was a bustle up and down the aisle as the passengers moved towards the forward door, where the stewardess struggled with the complicated handles. The man beside Stacey started to get up, and then sat back down again.

'You don't get off here? I thought it was the end of the line.'

'Not quite,' she sighed. 'They go on down to Temple, too. But I have to get off here. I don't want to, but I have to.'

'There's plenty of time. Relax.' He settled himself back in his seat as an example. 'This crowd will mill around for another ten minutes or so before the doorway is cleared. Cigarette?"

She shook her head, and the long thick blonde hair swung gently around her face, obscuring its soft creamy oval, and the grey eyes. 'I don't smoke,' she said, and then, driven by her fears, 'Why am I so scared? They can't make me marry him!'

'I suppose not,' he answered. 'Marry? Want to tell me about it?'

'I—no, I can't.' She turned her head away from him to hide the incipient tears. Why am I doing this? she screamed at herself. Why am I so—frightened? I never was like this before! Why so suddenly, in the past two years, have I become such a rabbit? They can't make me marry him, can they?

Outside her window she could see the other passengers straggling away from the aircraft, moving into the chill of the air-conditioned building. Now that the plane had stopped, the heat closed in on them, beating off the silver fuselage, and threatening to bake everything inside. The baggage handlers moved slowly, pulling luggage out of the belly compartment, tossing it carelessly on their battery-powered cart. Nobody else was in sight. For just a brief second Stacey felt elated. Maybe Uncle Henry couldn't come? But deep down, she knew better. It was a typical south Texas summer day, when even the crows were walking, but Uncle Henry would be there. Have no doubts about that, little lady!

'I wish I could just keep on flying,' she mused wearily. 'Just keep on going, and never come back. I wish I had a ticket to some place ten thousand miles from here.'

One of his hands came to her shoulder, the other offered a handkerchief. She snatched at it and dabbed her eyes before she turned to face him. 'I'll bet you think I'm a fool,' she suggested warily.

'No, not a fool,' he answered. His deep voice rumbled in the almost-empty aircraft. 'Just a scared kid. Look, my name is Harry. Sometimes it helps to talk to a complete stranger. If it would help you—?' The rest of the invitation floated on empty air as the stewardess came back to urge them off the plane. He stood up and moved out into the aisle to let her pass.

Stacey chewed her lip, watching the subtle movement

of his muscles as he slid away from her. It's no use delaying, she told herself. They'll be out there, waiting to pounce. And I might as well get it over. She was still shaking slightly, but having made her decision, she could feel the invidious effects of the pills take over, leaving her languid and dispirited. Like a condemned woman she stood up in the narrow space between the seats, brushed down her blue linen skirt, rearranged the simple lace-stippled blouse, and moved out into the aisle.

'Thank you,' she offered softly as she brushed by him and strode down the aisle. Her long slender legs wobbled as they carried her towards the exist, but her shoulders were squared, and she held herself as regally as any queen. If only I had the courage, she lectured herself. That's all I need, courage. I had it all once— Daddy called me his brave little girl. And look at me now! I'm the one who owns everything, not them! But as she stepped out of the gloom in the cabin into the bright sun, she knew very well that courage was exactly what she did not have.

Uncle Henry was not, as she had expected, standing at the foot of the ramp. Only the stewardess was there, holding her clipboard. The heat was like a slap in the face. A slight breeze brought in a touch of coolness from the lake. Stacey could almost see, almost taste Uncle Henry standing there. Somebody called from inside the terminal, and the sound reverberated off the aluminum skin of the airplane, and sent a shock wave through her. Her feet were frozen to the top stair, and she began to shake again. Good God, she screamed at herself, I'm coming apart at the seams! They can't do this to me. There *has* to be some place to run!

Warily, like a fox trapped in a covert, she backed slowly away from the rim of the stairs. One trembling step, and then another, before she backed into someone behind her, someone whose voice penetrated the fog of terror in her mind.

'There's nobody there!' Harry—the deep comforting

voice, the craggy comfortable face. Stacey whirled around and buried herself against his chest, still shaking. His welcome arms came around her again, warm and supporting.

'Here now!' He bent over to bring his lips close to her ears. 'Whoever they are, they're only people.' His lips teased the lobe of her ear.

'Not people—relatives.' He could hear the cry of anguish in her words, and a frown flashed over his face.

'Ah!' There seemed to be a million miles of under-standing in that one word. Her slender figure clung to him like a limpet. Both her arms went around his waist, as her eighteen years of shy reserve were dissolved by her immediate fear.

'Of course.' He offered her the handkerchief again, and gradually her stomach settled, and the tears stopped. He released his hold just enough so that she could wipe her eyes and blow her nose. 'Relax,' he instructed. 'Just look pretty. Leave everything else to me. We'll get our luggage. You are not to be afraid!'

It was like a command from on high. *You are not to be afraid.* And very suddenly it all seemed so simple. Of course—leave everything to him. I am *not* afraid. Do you hear that, Uncle Henry? I'm not afraid of you!

They went down the steps together, side by side, Harry's arm thrown protectively around her shoulders as he reduced his long stride to match hers. Halfway down he pulled her to a halt and turned her into his arms again. 'For the audience,' he whispered, as his head came down slowly over hers. His lips brushed hers casually, then returned, gently and warmly. As the pressure gradually increased, her arms stole upward, struggling around his neck. Her hands buried them-selves in the thick hair at the nape, pulling him into more intimate contact. Violently unclassified feelings ran up and down her spine, longings she knew from another life, perhaps. And when he broke the contact, she released her grip with strange reluctance.

'Remember now,' he cautioned her, 'let me do all the talking. You just look happy and pretty, smile a lot, and agree with everything I say, right?'

'I—yes,' she muttered, still deep in her daze. He fumbled with her left hand, and she felt cold metal against one of her fingers, then he was leading her down the stairs, with one arm hugging her closely.

They walked almost in lockstep across the steaming tarmac and fought their way inside, to the coolness of the air-conditioners. The luggage was already on display on the carousel. All their fellow passengers had disappeared. Outside Stacey could hear the engines of the commuter plane warm up again. Her eyes searched the terminal lobby. It was easy enough to stand on the stairs of the plane and say, I'm not afraid of you, Uncle Henry, but here on the flatland, moving closer and closer to meeting with him, was another story indeed.

She pointed out her single bag, and Harry pulled it off the carousel, along with two immaculate cowhide bags of his own. Gold initials sparked at her. HJM. I wonder what it means, one part of her mind asked, while the other directed her eyes into dark corners.

'Hey,' he said softly, and pulled her close, 'remember what I said.'

'I—I'm finding it hard to,' she stammered. 'I wish I had another pill!'

'Pills? At your age?' Another frown rode across his craggy face.

'Well, I—Aunt Ellen said I was—hyperactive, or something, and the pills—'

'Aunt Ellen?' he asked gruffly.

'She—my father's sister. She's my—my guardian, I guess.'

'Forget about the pills. Want anything here?'

What she wanted, she recognised, was not to go out that door. The lobby was empty of Delanos—any kind of Delano—which meant they must be waiting outside, in front. And all I want to do is stay in here, her conscience told her. 'A newspaper,' she muttered at Harry, for want of anything else to say.

He knew what she was up to, she could see, for a tiny smile played around the stern corners of his mouth. But his hand snatched up a copy of the *Waco Tribune-Herald*, and tucked it under her arm. 'Nothing else?'

'I—' Courage is what I need, she told herself desperately. There's no time for lesser measures. 'Would you kiss me again?'

His tiny smile became a wide grin. 'It's addictive,' he said softly as he leaned down and administered another one, like the first, but longer this time. Stacey's hands refused to release him until she had run completely out of breath. Her feet were inches off the floor, and her head miles above—or at least it seemed that way. When he finally dropped her, she could feel the warm imprint of his hand on the middle of her back, as if he had branded her for life. She leaned her head against his chest, just long enough to catch her breath. When he pushed her slightly away she could see he was laughing— not at her, but from the joy of it all.

'You surprise me,' he chuckled. 'And I thought I'd done it all!'

She dared not ask what he meant. She bowed her head and ducked behind her swinging hair, using her fingers to bring everything back to its normally pristine fall. It was all an excuse, an attempt to give herself time to sort out her startled emotions, which refused to be sorted. Nothing like this had ever happened to her before. Nothing.

'Your ghosts aren't here?' He was searching the terminal himself.

'They're bound to be,' she sighed, coming back down to earth with a thud. 'They wouldn't let me—'

'They wouldn't let you run free?'

'I—Aunt Ellen is all the relative I've got.' It startled her to find herself defending her aunt, even in so small a way. But old habits died hard, and up until the time she married Uncle Henry, three years ago, Aunt Ellen had been as fair and kind and understanding as a bitter woman could be.

'You've got more now,' he said enigmatically. 'Remember what I told you. Smile a lot, and look pretty, but keep your mouth shut. Right?'

'I—right. Yes, sir. My dad was an Army Colonel. You sound a lot like him.'

'I shouldn't be surprised,' he chuckled. 'Buckle up and prepare to jump.' That strong arm came down around her waist again, instilling courage by osmosis, right through the thin linen of her dress. Stacey savoured it, rebuilding her stock of bravery. When Harry turned her loose and picked up the bags instead, she felt bereft, like the little girl who expected a lollipop from the bank teller, and got only a smile.

So they continued towards the outer doors, and the car park. She moved with a mixture of bravado and tremor, putting a good face on things, so to speak, but ready to jump at a second's notice—and praying there would be at least a second.

With both hands full, Harry backed into the glass doors and held them open for her to pass through. She was smiling her thanks when she heard the roar behind her.

'Well, it's about time,' growled Uncle Henry. 'You've kept us waiting in the hot sun for over thirty minutes!'

Stacey cringed. The first lash of the whip. She knew what he meant. Stacey Bronfield was responsible not only for keeping them waiting, but also for the hot sun itself, and the humidity, and his discomfort at having to drive all the way to Waco from clear on the other side of Gatesville. And there was just a little threat behind it, too. Like, wait until I get you home, girl!

Very suddenly Stacey realised that even this strong man—this Harry—could hardly cope with Uncle Henry. And, dear God, George was right behind him. Uncle Henry's voice had been fine-tuned by years of hell-raising. It had the sharp bray of a startled Texas mule. Uncle Henry. Superimpose what he used to be over what he is now, and see the difference. He's dressed in the best clothes money can buy—my money, Stacey noted grimly. A lightweight white summer suit, boots— as if he ever dared to come near a horse—and an expensive ten-gallon hat. Just under six feet, going to seed at the waistline. A sallow face; despite claiming to be a Texan, Uncle Henry hated to go out in the sun. And behind him, a thinner carbon copy, his son George. Except for the hat. George was proud of his shoulder-length fair hair. And where his father's face was planed and furrowed by life, George's was as smooth as a baby's bottom.

'And so this is your family?' Harry squeezed her shoulders gently, just enough to shake her out of her stupor. He had dropped the bags, and was standing with feet slightly spread, his hawk-eyes scanning the pair in front of them. Under his breath she heard him render the final Texas judgment. 'Dudes,' he muttered.

He didn't wait for her to answer. He moved directly in front of Uncle Henry, between Stacey and her relatives, close enough so that her uncle was forced to bend his head back a little to look up at him. 'I'm Harry,' he boomed, extending a hand towards Stacey. 'Harry Marsden, you know.'

The two other men stared blankly at him. It's the first time I've ever seen Uncle Henry faced down, Stacey thought, and the very idea restored some of her compo-sure. A tiny giggle bubbled in her throat, and almost made it to the outside world. Almost. His next statement rocked her back on her heels.

'Harry Marsden,' he repeated in that deep booming voice. 'Kitten's new husband.'

Uncle Henry stepped back as if he had been stung by a scorpion. He opened his mouth to say something, but only managed to gasp like a gaffed fish. George, who looked like a child watching someone steal his ice cream, took two threatening steps forward. Stacey swallowed her giggle and tried her best not to choke on it—or him.

'You mean you—you and Stacey—' stuttered Uncle Henry. His face was turning a brilliant sunset red. 'You two?'

'Right in one gasp,' Harry returned, laughing. 'Stacey and I. Us two. Isn't it wonderful?' He turned back to her, and pulled her close again, tilting her chin up with one of his huge fingers. 'It *is* wonderful, isn't it, Kitten?'

'I—yes. Yes, it's wonderful.' Stacey's confidence was improving by leaps and bounds. There was no doubt about it; he could do it. He was doing it! 'Magical. It's so wonderful that it's almost unbelievable!' There was a warning twinkle in those dark eyes that shut her mouth with a snap. Look pretty, keep your mouth shut, she commanded. Things were bad enough with two Delanos mad at her, without adding a—what had he said?—a Marsden to the list. And doesn't that sound nice? Harry Marsden. Harry J. Marsden. Mrs Stacey Marsden? It did have a nice ring to it. Where have I heard that name before? she wondered. And then he was lifting up her left hand in front of Uncle Henry's nose.

'There, you see,' he stated flatly. 'Signed, sealed, and delivered. Until death do us part, and all that.' Uncle Henry gasped again. Glaring in the summer sun was one of the largest diamonds Stacey had ever seen—a garish old-fashioned thing, surrounded with diamond chips, set in a platinum ring. Which was an exact match for the ornate platinum wedding ring that squirrelled down next to it on Stacey's finger.

George pushed his father aside, making noises deep in his throat, his arms outstretched as if he meant death to them part at just that very moment, or at least within the next five. Harry watched him come with an inane smile on his lips. Then at the last moment he pushed Stacey to one side, moved both his arms rapidly in front of him, and very suddenly George was sitting down on the sidewalk, his nose slightly bent, and a trickle of blood streaming down from it.

'You hit him!' Stacey gasped at the audacity of this man who had claimed her as his bride.

'Yes, I do seem to have,' Harry returned coolly. 'Bruised my knuckles, too. A stupid thing to do, but sort of automatic. A karate chop would have been better—knuckles are at best a poor thing to hit out with. I need a little sympathy, Kitten.'

'I—you hit George!' Stacey's head was buzzing with the notion. Lord, how many times have I wanted to hit George, she told herself. How many times? And Harry had just put out his hand and—hit him!

'Well, it did seem to be the thing to do,' he rumbled. 'He was being pretty offensive. Was there anybody else who needs hitting, while I'm in the mood?'

Uncle Henry had lived by his wits for a long time, and he quickly shifted the conflict into the verbal level. 'Surely you don't expect us to believe all this nonsense,' he stormed. 'Stacey was not married when she got on that plane! Get over here, girl. We're going home—immediately! Do you hear?'

Stacey's robot legs almost carried her forward, but Harry's arm intervened, wrapping her up in his protective cocoon again. 'She's going home all right,' Harry said coldly. 'With me. And while we're at it, just who the hell are you?'

'Why—why—' Uncle Henry spluttered, 'I'm her uncle, of course.'

'Only by marriage,' Stacey interjected.

'I'm her guardian,' continued Uncle Henry. 'I'm responsible for her welfare.' And then the older man's courage reasserted itself. 'And now I'll ask you to get your hands off her—at once, do you hear?'

'I've got plans for keeping my hands on this girl for the next fifty years,' drawled Harry. 'And just what makes you think you're Stacey's guardian?'

'Why, I—I'm married to her aunt, her only living

relative. She's my wife's brother's daughter.'

'You talk as if you thought she was under age, friend. Whatever gave you that idea?'

'Idea? Why, of course she is. She's seventeen.' Uncle Henry was caught in the grip of a terrible rage, with no safe outlet in sight. Stacey could see the red gleam in his eyes, but she could not let the untruth stand.

'It isn't so, Harry. I'm eighteen. Three months ago I was eighteen!'

'And so that would seem to put an end to your guardianship, if it ever existed,' said Harry grimly. 'In fact, it would seem to require an accounting of your stewardship, Mr—?'

'Delano,' stuttered Uncle Henry. He's going to burst a blood vessel any minute, Stacey told herself. And as terrible as it sounds, I think I would be glad. 'Henry Delano,' her uncle repeated. 'And I have Stacey's power of attorney, all signed and sealed under the law.'

'A waste of paper,' Harry told him. 'In Texas everything changes when the lady marries. Now, about that accounting?'

'What accounting?'

'You know,' snapped Harry. 'A legal statement telling us what you've done with her property and money. Pretty simple, isn't it? And as her husband I'll represent Stacey in any future debates of this nature. You do have a lawyer?'

'I don't need a lawyer!' Uncle Henry was still trying to bluster it out, but with only half the fervour he usually employed.

'You need a lawyer very badly, Mr Delano. Here it is Friday. On Monday Kitten and I will come over to check up on your trusteeship. Where do I find you?'

'At Rancho Miraflores,' interjected Stacey. 'Just west of Gatesville. It's mine. They all just—moved in. They—' Harry raised his hand and stopped her in mid-sentence.

'Then they'd better be prepared to move out just as

quickly,' he said. Then, without waiting for the Delanos to say anything, he took Stacey's arm and led her in the direction of the parking lot. She found herself staggering, as if her two-inch heels were too high—or as if her shoulders had just been relieved of a massive burden. He felt her wobble, and swept her up in his arms, as if she were a small child. All at once she felt tired. Reaction was setting in from the massive struggle that had taken place within her, and she was worn to the nub. 'Don't let it all get to you, Kitten,' Harry murmured in her ear.

'I—it's hard not to,' she whispered back, feeling a joy at the warmth of him, the strength, the assurance.

It was a Mercedes 280XL into which he ushered her, propping her up on the soft seat and strapping her in with a safety belt. As he walked around the front of the car she settled herself against the back of the seat and watched. That's what it is, she told herself. He doesn't walk—he just seems to flow along the ground like some jungle cat. And I don't really know whether he's done me some good, or just made things worse, do I?

The seat sank as he climbed in. 'Just hold on a minute,' he said. He started the motor, waited until it was running smoothly, then flipped on the air-conditioner. Moments later cool air flowed out of multiple vents straight at her, ruffling her hair, whispering at the hem of her dress.

'Now then, tell me all about it.' His invitation was extended behind a warm smile. It changed his face from a craggy silhouette to something almost good-looking. Almost—the qualification brought a smile to her lips, and set her nose to wrinkling.

'Like Peter Rabbit,' he commented. 'Tell me.'

'You mean about them?'

'Well, more than likely I mean about you, and then about them. Start at the beginning and go forward.'

Stacey almost said, 'Yes, sir.' And she did mentally click her heels. 'Well, in the beginning there was my dad and I,' she started, then stopped to lick her lips, and think.

'Don't do that,' chuckled Harry. 'You act like a girl who needs to be kissed. And what happened to your mother?'

She shrank farther into her corner of the car and watched him apprehensively. That second kiss had been so startling that she was afraid of what another might bring!

'I—I didn't do anything on purpose,' she said shyly. 'I guess I had a mother, but I don't remember her. She died when I was born. It was always just me and my dad.'

'All right, I'll settle for that. There was you and your dad. And then what happened?'

'Daddy—he was a soldier, you know. And he owned a ranch. He was an officer in the regular Army. He flew helicopters, and things like that. And when they sent him someplace and I couldn't go, he would take me up to St Anselm's, the convent school in Dallas, and leave me there until he came back. And then he was ordered to Vietnam, and he didn't come back.'

'Oh, wow! How old were you then?'

'I was—I was thirteen when he left. Fourteen when they sent the word that he couldn't come back.'

'And then Aunt Ellen came. She was different then. She took me out of the school, and we went to the ranch.'

'What school did you go to then?'

'Why, no school. We just lived at the ranch, Aunt Ellen and I. She was my father's sister. Did I say that before? She had no money of her own, and she was— well, you'll see for yourself. I never did understand it. Daddy was a handsome man. Aunt Ellen, she looks like—But it was nice on the ranch. I helped with the stock—we ran beef. It was before they—well, just before. And we were happy, Aunt Ellen and I. Then Henry Delano came along. He took one look at my aunt, two at the ranch, and they got married.'

'You don't care for your uncle?' queried Harry.

'I—he—he tried to—touch me,' she said reluctantly.

'Oh damn! One of that kind!'

'It wasn't terribly bad. It's a very big ranch, and I could keep out of his sight pretty easily. But then, when I was sixteen, he found out somehow that all the property belonged to me, and Aunt Ellen hadn't anything. That made him terribly angry at both of us. And that's when George appeared.'

'Ah! George is Uncle Henry's son—a Delano?'

'Yes. He had been married a good many years before—I think. At least, he said George was his son.'

'All right, you needn't tell me the rest. They all decided that you ought to marry George. Right?'

'Yes. How did you know?'

'It wasn't hard.' Harry laughed, but it was a cold glittering laugh, with no warmth in it at all.

'They just kept after me, morning noon and night,' Stacey went on. '*You ought to marry George, Stacey*. Or, *you have to marry George, Stacey*. Things like that. And then—lord, he would chase me too. Only there was one thing in my favour. George is afraid of horses, so if I could get to the stables I was always safe. And then—' She was fighting to keep the tears out of her voice, and having very little luck. 'And then they said I should go to Dallas to sign some legal papers—and when I came back I would have to marry George!'

'So why didn't you just disappear?'

'With what?' she asked scornfully. 'You can see what I am. I don't have the courage to go out on my own, and I don't have a penny to my name. Look at me! They laugh and call me the little heiress, and look—' she fumbled in her purse, 'I've got ten, twenty, forty-six cents to my name. Where would I run to? What would I do? I don't know a thing about anything except horses.'

'And you've not been to school since you were fourteen?'

'Not a day. I read a lot, but that's not schooling.' Her

words fumbled away through softness to inaudibility, until finally she ground to a halt. Why didn't I run away? She asked herself. Why couldn't I work up enough courage to do something about my own life? Why?

An uncomfortable silence fell over them, with only the purr of the engine and the high-pitched whine of the air-conditioner to fill the void. One of Harry's hands moved across the back of the seat and settled at the nape of her neck, massaging it gently.

'Poor kid.' Oh, my God, thought Stacey, now he's going to *pity* me. I don't want that. Anything but pity—anything! I'd almost rather go back to Uncle Henry.

He felt the tension in her neck muscles. 'Don't fight it,' he said gently. 'Relax.'

'Why did you say that?' she asked.

'Say what?'

'That we—that—we were married?'

'Hey, that was a little far-fetched, wasn't it?' he chuckled. 'But we had to give them some surprise—and you'll admit it worked.'

'For the moment.' She smiled, reflecting on the look on Uncle Henry's face. And George! 'I thought George was going to fall through the ground!' But then the serious side of it came back to her.

'But it only delayed things, you know. Sooner or later I have to go back home. And they'll all be there—and then what's going to happen?'

'A great deal of what's going to happen depends entirely on you, Kitten,' returned Harry.

'Why do you keep calling me Kitten?'

'That's another story, Stacey. Maybe I'll tell you about it one of these days. But first, let's stick to you. What do you want to have happen? Would you like me to go with you on Monday and talk to the Delanos again? To get them off your ranch? Can you run the ranch without them?'

'It—it doesn't take any running,' she admitted softly. 'We don't run cattle any more. Four years ago they—

somebody—found oil on our land. Everything is run by Parsons Oil Company now, under a lease. We just have the house, and about three hundred acres. They lease the rest. And—'

'And what?'

'Would you really go with me?'

'Would you like me to?'

Would I like to walk up the front stairs, and see them standing there, and me with my arm through his? Would I like to see him roar at them and make them shiver the way they've made me? Would I like that!

'Yes, I think I would like that very much,' she said happily.

'It will cost you something,' he chuckled. 'There's a fee.'

'I—I guess if I—I suppose there must be some money in my bank account, if—you wouldn't charge too much?'

'Oh, I charge a great deal, Kitten. But it's not money I want from you, you know.'

'I know? How could I know? But I do want you—I have to have you come with me, or I can't go myself. So tell me, what's your price?'

'Very simple,' he said solemnly now, his dark eyes following every movement of her facial muscles. 'I want you to come with me to my grandmother's house, and spend the weekend pretending that you're my wife!'

CHAPTER TWO

STACEY looked over at him, her eyes wide, her mouth pursed. 'To be your wife? To—I don't understand.' Very suddenly the car had become overwhelmingly chilled, as if a cloud had obscured the bright sun. *To be your wife? What he means is he wants me to—to share a bed with him for the weekend. And I thought he was my own true knight. Hah!*

'Did you know your lips move when you talk to yourself?' he asked.

'Hah!' *It seemed impossible to find anything else to say. I'm so tired—so tired. He wants me to be his temporary wife. What a nice name for such a mean position! He wants a weekend mistress, and like all those older men, he wants somebody young. I should feel damn angry about it, shouldn't I? Then how come I just feel—sleepy?? And my ears are buzzing so?*

'What kind of pills were those your aunt gave you?' demanded Harry.

The question was right out of the blue. It was the last subject in the world she expected. 'I don't know,' she mumbled sleepily. 'There were all kinds—some little white ones, and then some yellow ones, and then some blue ones. I never asked the name, because—' *Because I can't hold my head up for another minute. Aunt Ellen gave me two of the blue ones this morning, and I haven't the strength to talk any more.*

Slowly, like the Tower of Pisa, she began to lean over towards him. She was fast asleep when her head finally landed on his shoulder and slipped off. He cradled it with one hand, moving back against the seat to make a little pocket where she could rest. She sighed in her dreaming, and shifted over beside him, both hands wrapped around his upper arm. Her feet came up off the floor and on to the seat. Unconsciously she tucked them up under her, and settled her entire weight on him, in a graceful half-kneeling position. Her lips parted slightly; he could hear the rhythmic passage of air. She wiggled once or twice, squirming closer as she did, then was still.

He sat perfectly still until he was sure she was sound asleep. It was hard to keep the satisfied smile off his face. There was no doubt about it, she was perfect for the part. True, except for the hair, she had only the vaguest similarity to Lisette. But Grandmother was almost totally blind. And it was the aura about her, not her looks, that had struck him. Not that she wasn't a beauty—for that she certainly was. An innocent beauty, full of spirit and loveliness, and that was something that Lisette never was! It *would* work. It had to work. There wasn't time for another search, another replacement.

His left hand tapped at the steering wheel of the car as he assessed her. Five foot seven, perhaps eight? Lovely hair. The hand that had been on her shoulder moved up and toyed with the fullness of it. Strange, he thought, there are lighter streaks in it. I wonder how she does that? Thick curly eyelashes. Eighteen? She'll set the male world on fire by the time she's twenty-one. Green eyes, weren't they? Or grey? It had been hard to tell, with the crying and all. A slender figure, tall for a girl. Nice hips, well rounded. Magnificent breasts! Lord, come on, Harry, the kid's too young for you, and too full of fears. Get on with the masquerade, then get her home. That pair of dudes who thought they could milk the child of all her money were in for some surprise! He had to use his left hand to reach the stick-shift of the automatic drive; using his right would surely wake her up. It cost an extra two dollars to get the parking attendant to put their bags in the back seat of the car. He whistled under his breath as he drove out on to Airport Road, then turned north on Rock Creek road.

Stacey napped for twenty minutes or so, then came brightly awake. The car was bumping down a potholed farm-to-market road. For a moment or two, wide awake, she savoured the comfort, and nuzzled closer to him. Then she began to think, and instantly her peaches-and-cream complexion turned a brilliant red. She pushed herself up and moved back into the farthest corner of the car, stammering her apologies.

'No need,' Harry laughed softly. 'I enjoyed it all.' He flexed his right arm a few times. 'Even my arm went to sleep. Feel better?'

'Yes. Where are we?' A soft, almost timid request from someone who obviously was not allowed to do much questioning. The tone cut him, leaving behind a swift sweet pain that had nothing to do with pity.'

'About a quarter of a mile from my grandmother's home,' he answered. 'About eight miles north of Waco.' He was still flexing his right hand and fingers as he pulled over to the shoulder of the road and stopped the big car. When the emergency brake was set he turned sidewise in the seat to give her his full attention. 'You said you couldn't go home alone?'

She nodded agreement.

'And you would like me to go with you to de-louse the place?'

Stacey giggled uncontrollably. 'We still have some cattle-dip in the barm,' she finally managed to get out. 'Is that good on humans?'

'Calm down,' he sighed. 'It was an unfortunate choice of words.' He settled himself back in the seat and watched her face intently. 'We'll go over there on Monday, and I'll stay long enough to get everything straightened out to your satisfaction.'

'You're a lawyer?' Her eyes widened at the thought. The only lawyers she knew were cold business types who lived in Dallas.

'No,' he interrupted her train of thought, 'but I have a couple of lawyers working for me. Not to worry—it's the weekend between now and Monday I want to talk about.'

'Oh.' He could see her face drop. The dimple on her left cheek disappeared, to be replaced by a tic that pulled at the corner of her mouth. 'I'm—not sure I can pay your price.' The words rattled out at full speed, as if she were eager to get them out and gone. 'I—I don't have any experience in this sort of thing.' She was trembling, almost uncontrollably.

'Of course you don't, child.' There was a snap in his voice that brought her head up. Anger? she thought, I'm the one who ought to be insulted, and *he's* angry?

'Look here,' he said, 'this is strictly a business proposition, nothing more. You're too young for me, little lady.'

For some reason the comment stung her. Too young? Hah! She pulled her shoulders back and took a deep breath. And I hope that bugs your eyes out, her mind shouted at him. But his eyes stayed glued to her face, and how long can you hold your breath just to look sexy? She let the air escape in a wild sigh, and slumped down.

'That's better.' There was a paternal chuckle in his voice. 'Now, Stacey, I went to Dallas to hire an actress to do an impersonation for me, but I couldn't find anyone suitable. Until I met you on the plane, that is.'

'You want an actress? I don't know anything about acting.'

'That's what makes you perfect for the part.'

She looked up at him, measured what she saw, and was satisfied. 'OK,' she said, 'tell me about it.'

'It's my grandmother,' Harry began. 'She's eighty-five, and living in the old family home just around that bend in front of us. She's dying, Stacey. The doctors tell me that she'll be lucky to make it through the weekend. And she's dying troubled.' He stopped long enough to search her face again. Then, apparently satisfied with what he saw, he continued.

'My grandmother raised me from a pup. Me and Lisette Langloise, her godchild. Grandmother always expected Lisette and me to marry, but that never set right with me. Anyway, a bigger fish swam into sight, and Lisette departed, for parts unknown, as they say. That was eight years ago, and Grandmother still grieves. I want her to go with a clear mind. And that's where you come in.'

'You want me to make believe we're married, and that I'm Lisette? Do I look like her or something?'

'Not a bit,' he chuckled, 'which is a mark in your favour, believe me. Don't worry about that—Grandmother is blind, slightly deaf, and completely bedridden. I'll present you to her, you'll wear Lisette's favourite perfume, and we'll play it by ear. Love is what she needs, and you look like what she romanticises Lisette to be. You're almost exactly Grandmother's dream. Well?'

It was a request that Stacey could not possibly refuse, and yet she stalled. 'There won't be any—I—being your wife—there won't be any hanky-panky?'

'Hanky-panky?' Harry threw back his head and roared. 'I didn't know people actually talked like that these days,' he gurgled. 'No, Kitten, there won't be any hanky-panky. There are three other people in the house, and outside Grandmother's bedroom everything will be as decorous as one of the Mayor's lawn parties—which are plenty boring, let me tell you. Well?'

She waited a moment, hoping that her mind would throw up some well-reasoned excuses. But none came. Her mind remained an absolute blank. And Harry's craggy face had an appeal on it that said more than words. Why he's not actually homely, she told herself. 'Yes,' she said.

'Yes? No yes but. Or yes and?'

'No. When I make up my mind I don't quibble. It's just yes.'

'Thank God for you,' he said as he started the engine.

'What in the world have I been doing, fooling around with all those other women?'

The car started forward, bumping back on to the road surface. 'Waiting around for me to grow up?' suggested Stacey, in that wicked humour that found so few places for expression. He grinned at her, then turned his attention to the road.

A few yards farther on they swept around a bend in the road, and there on a hill in front of them, surrounded by carefully fenced paddocks, was the house. It towered above the landscape in a Victorian mishmash of dormers, gables, and towers, two stories high, with a huge curved veranda enveloping everything.

'I thought you had a ranch!' gasped Stacey. 'It looks just like the old Cooper home in the city!'

'An exact copy,' he laughed, 'built a year later, in 1908. My great-grandfather built it for his immigrant wife. Come on in.'

She followed him slowly up the stairs, through the door with the inset stained glass windows, and down the hall. A middle-aged woman, black hair turning white, bustled out of the door behind the stairs. 'We're back, Millie,' said Harry, and the woman stopped, hiding her hands under her apron.

'I'm all flour and chocolate,' she laughed. 'And this is—?'

Stacey could hear him take a deep breath, as if preparing to make a deep dive. 'This is my wife, Millie. We were married in Dallas. Stacey, this is Millie Fallon, who runs the house. Her husband Frank does everything else that's required.'

'Your wife? You mean you finally did it? Oh, Harry, wait until your grandmother hears!' There were tears in the older woman's eyes, and she lifted a corner of her apron to wipe them off. 'Welcome home, Mrs Marsden.'

'Please, call me Stacey. "Mrs Marsden" is a little too much for me to handle right this minute!'

'Of course—Stacey. A nice round name. You come from these parts?'

'Over Gatesville way. We have a little ranch over there.'

'Harry—you'd better get yourself and your surprise package upstairs,' said Millie. 'The nurse came down for your grandmother's meal a few minutes ago. Lunch could be ready in—say, fifteen minutes, Stacey?'

'I—' Stacey fumbled for words. Is this what a wife is supposed to do? she thought. I suppose it must be, but what do I say? She looked over to Harry for some signal. He was grinning at her, one eyelid barely dropped, an almost imperceptible wink.

'Oh, that would be fine—Millie?' With both of them beaming at her she felt an access of strength, and was almost jovial as Harry tucked one hand under her elbow and urged her up the stairs.

The ground floor halls and rooms had been bright with light, flashing with colours. Here on the upper floor everything was in shaded darkness, lit by tiny safety lights spaced down the hall about four inches above the floor. He led her down to an empty bedroom at the end of the hall. The curtains were open, so the eternal gloom of the hallway was relieved. Stacey looked around in surprise. Gold on white was the motif—frilly white, loaded with lace. Certainly not a man's room!

'Yours?' she ventured cautiously, and he laughed, an uproarious guffaw. 'Not hardly. Now where the devil is that—ah, here.' He had been searching the low dressing table in the corner, and came back to her with a perfume bottle.

'This was Lisette's room,' he explained. 'Grandmother kept it clean and ready for her—being sure she would be back, you know. Here's the perfume.'

Stacey took the stoppered bottle from him, still looking around the room. What a disaster of a bedroom! It looks more like a harem than a sleeping place, she told herself.

'Well?' Harry interrupted her train of thought.

'I—well what?'

'The perfume—put it on. It's the one thing Grandma will recognise right away.'

'Put it on?' she queried.

'Oh, come on now, don't tell me you've never used perfume before!'

'All right,' she told him, feeling miserable about it, 'I won't tell you that.' But I haven't, she screamed silently at him. I don't even know where to start!

He showed his impatience for two minutes, then took the bottle back and pulled out the stopper. 'Like this,' he sighed. He dabbed at her wrists, the pulse point in her neck, and behind the lobes of her ears, then he stepped back to measure the result. 'Okay, you smell fine. Remember, you're Lisette, and she's your godmother, and you've been away for eight years. Ready?'

'I don't think I'll ever be ready,' stammered Stacey. 'I'm really not an actress—you must know that.' And besides, the perfume was almost overpowering her with its musky undertones.

'I know, but don't let that worry you. Just do what comes naturally.' His long lean hand swallowed her wrist, and he towed her out into the corridor and down to the third door from the stairs. It opened just as they came abreast of it, and a woman dressed in nurse's uniform came out—a small woman, overly round, with freckles across her nose, and a big smile.

'She's just finished her lunch,' the nurse whispered. 'I think she'll want to rest for a while. You could have perhaps fifteen minutes, no longer. She's really down in the dumps.'

'I've got the cure for that,' whispered Harry in return. He patted Stacey's wrist, still entangled in his hand-trap. 'Stacey, this is Nurse Wilson—Sara to her friends. Sara, my wife Stacey.'

The nurse's smile turned into a broad grin. She stepped out into the hall and closed the door behind her. 'Wonderful,' she crowed. 'Marvellous! Is this the girl she calls Kitten?'

'This is she. She is it—whatever. Why don't you go get your lunch, and let us see what sort of miracle we can concoct up here.' The nurse nodded, and pushed them both towards the door. Harry turned the knob and gestured Stacey ahead of him, but she stopped in the middle of the door-jamb. 'So that's why!' she hissed at him.

'Why what?'

'Why you keep calling me Kitten. It was *her* name!'

'Yes, it was the name we all used.'

'Don't you ever call me that again,' she said fiercely. 'Not ever again!'

'Why, I do believe you're jealous!'

'No such a thing. But don't you dare call me that again!'

He wasn't prepared to fight, not on the threshold of his grandmother's bedroom. One of his huge hands settled in the middle of her back and pushed her into the room.

A small bedlamp provided the only light. The scent of flowers filled the air. An air-conditioner hummed songs to itself in the corner. The bed was an old four-poster, raised on blocks to the height of a regular hospital bed, and the little stick-figure lay exactly in the middle of it, with back and head raised on double pillows. As the pair of them ghosted across the thick carpet, Stacey studied the recumbent form.

A thin face, almost fallen in, that spoke of past beauty. White hair, growing sparse in spots, but still kept in curl for pride's sake. A long white nightgown, with a choker collar, and a tiny bit of blue ribbon at neck and wrists. Long beautiful hands, translucent skin over thin bones, with touches of brown pigmentation spots. Only the hands moved, clutching and unclutching the sheet that covered her. Occasionally the eyes blinked, but their faded blue saw nothing.

Stacey gasped. Raised without elderly people around her, she was instantly touched by this tiny relic. 'Who's there?' the voice quavered—halfway between a handsome contralto and a squeak.

'It's me, Harry,' he said quietly, leaning over to drop a light kiss on the clear forehead. 'I've brought you a surprise.'

'A surprise?' Both eyes popped open, and one thin hand reached out towards his. 'Harry, you're enough of a surprise for—what's that smell? Lilacs? Harry!'

'Yes, love.' Strange how soft his voice was, Stacey thought as she watched; you could almost feel the caressing love in it. 'She's come back, Grandma—Kitten's back. And that's only half the surprise.'

'Half?' The hand groped away from him, reaching blindly into the darkness. Compelled by an emotion she had never felt before—not pity, but something deeper—Stacey took the searching hand in her own. The fingers intertwined with hers, strongly for a woman so ill. And then both hands shifted to Stacey's left, and explored.

'Kitten!' The words were like a sigh running down the wind. 'It's been so long, my darling. But you've come home. I can go in peace, my love, and—Kitten? You're wearing my mother's rings? You and Harry?'

'Yes,' he said, from just over her shoulder. 'Lisette and I. Does that make you happy, Grandmother?'

Tiny tears rolled out from under the shuttered eyes and ran down the hollows of the sunken cheeks. 'The Lord has been good to me,' the old woman muttered, then was silent.

'She's fallen asleep,' Harry whispered in Stacey's ear. 'That's the way it goes. We might as well go down to lunch.'

Stacey made an attempt to free her hand, but met instant objection from the reclining woman. 'No,' his grandmother whispered. 'It's been so long. Stay with me, Kitten.'

'Of course,' she murmured softly. Some memory,

some emotion, drove her to lean over the bed and kiss the tear-stained cheek. 'Of course I will.' She gestured with her head. Harry brought up a comfortable chair to the bedside, and she dropped into it, still holding the fragile hand in her own. 'You go along and have your lunch,' she told him. 'I'll stay as long as she needs me.'

'Sara will be back in an hour,' he promised. 'Come downstairs when she comes in.'

'If your grandmother wants me to,' Stacey returned, and could not for the life of her reason out why she had said that. At nine o'clock she had been in Dallas, saying goodbye to Aunt Ellen, swallowing her pills *like a good little girl*. And here it was just after midday, and she was sitting in a strange house, at the bedside of a strangely loveable woman. And a man who called her his wife was standing behind her, giving orders. Out of the maze of all this confusion something good might come. So I'll sit here and see if I can sort it all out, she thought. The hand enclosed in hers squeezed lightly. She returned the gesture, and looked around to find that her 'husband' had gone.

The nurse did return at one o'clock, but the patient's restless sleep would not allow a disengagement, so it was three that afternoon before Stacey managed the stairs, and found her way into the living room where Harry was waiting. He put down his paper and got up, welcoming her with a brief hug. 'Thank you, Stacey,' he said, in that same soft caressing voice he had used with his grandmother. 'I came up twice to check. It worked! Hungry?'

'I think I'm starving.' She flexed her arm and hand to restore the circulation. At the same time Millie bustled in with a plate of sandwiches. 'Coffee?' the housekeeper asked.

'Milk?' Stacey suggested timidly, and both of them smiled at each other over her head.

'Milk, of course.' Millie smiled again and went back to the kitchen, singing. Stacey consumed two sandwiches in short order, drank down the milk thirstily, then turned around to Harry. 'You've got a dribble of milk on your chin,' he told her. 'Come on, we'll take a walk around the area. You sure need some exercise.' Of course I do, she mumbled to herself. I need food, I need exercise, I need—why is the world so full of people willing to tell me what I need? What I really need is—whatever in the world am I thinking of! She made a hasty swipe at her chin, and almost ran to catch up to him. Strange, too—she felt as if she were floating over the ground, never touching.

He led her out of the back door into a lush green world that took her breath away. Long paddocks, fenced in white-painted wood, stretched in all directions. In one, several mares, each with a foal, cropped lazily. In the far opposite, resting in the shade of an old oak tree, a brilliant white stallion took his ease.

'I don't understand any of this,' said Stacey, her interest caught both by the animals and the land. 'Over most of middle Texas there's hardly a blade of green grass. Everything is sere and brown. And those magnificent animals! Morgans?'

'That's why my great-grandfather built here on the hill.' Harry was pointing towards a low concrete structure behind the house, with pipes running out in all directions. 'It's a fresh water spring—never been known to fail, in over eighty years, although it does get a little brackish sometimes in the August droughts. And no, they're not Morgans. Those are thoroughbred Arabs, every one of them.'

'Arabs? They're so beautiful. So that's what you do for a living!'

'Don't say that too loudly,' he chuckled. 'There's a spy from the Internal Revenue Service behind every tree these days! Actually, raising blooded Arabs has been a fine tax shelter for many years. People raise them for the tax loss, you understand.'

She didn't, but she hated to tell him so. 'But you?'

'But, with a little concentration, and a lot of luck, I

manage to make a profit. No, little lady, I make my living downtown in Waco. I have a little building on Clay Avenue, near the University. All this out here belongs to my grandmother—except the Arabs.'

'Oh.' It wasn't much of a conversational gambit, but it was all she could muster. Her heart had run out to the foals, and to the little old woman upstairs, and to—but I don't intend to think about *that*, she lectured herself. I'll think about that when I get home.

'Funny, isn't it,' she said, meaning funny-strange, not funny-ha-ha, 'I've got oil on my property, and your grandmother has water. I wish we could trade.'

He chuckled at her, lifting her chin up with his index finger. 'What big eyes you have,' he teased. 'And that's the problem with a great deal of Texas—there's plenty of water, but not where we want it. Come on, let's go down to the stables and look around.'

They dined together that night, sitting close together at a huge round table that almost filled the dining room. 'It seats twenty,' he told Stacey when she enquired. 'Steak, mashed potatoes, tortillas? Mrs Fallon favours Mexican food; most of the hands are *vaqueros*.'

'I don't mind,' laughed Stacey, and thought to herself, that's the first time I can remember really laughing since Daddy—since all those years ago! It's just so—pleasant—being Mrs Harry Marsden. No wonder Aunt Ellen rushed into marriage! I *must* not judge Aunt Ellen too harshly. I wonder if I should have my pills now?

She asked him, right in the middle of a bite, and his fork clattered down to the table with a thump, and he leaned over towards her. 'I don't think you need any pills!' he thundered. Oh Lord, she thought, it's like pronouncements from Mount Sinai. I hope he doesn't throw lightning bolts at people who displease him. Or do I have the wrong mountain?

'I—I just—' she stammered. 'Aunt Ellen said I was hyperactive, and had to have them, and I'm getting a very peculiar feeling in—'

'That's enough of that subject!' Harry returned, somewhere between a shout and a roar. And of course that's it, Stacey told herself warily as she ducked her head towards her plate and tried to hide behind her mass of hair. He roars—but somehow he doesn't frighten me the way Uncle Henry does. Maybe all men roar at their women? *Their* women? What a lovely thought that was getting to be. She struggled to suppress the secret smile that flirted at the corners of her mouth, as she spooned up the last of the potatoes, and the rich brown gravy that covered them.

After dinner Harry took her back upstairs again, and into the darkened room. A new nurse was on duty, and she held her hand to her lips and shushed them as they came in. 'She's asleep,' she whispered.

'No, she's not,' the voice quavered from the bed. 'Kitten? Come and sit by me again.'

Stacey laughed at the astonishment written on the nurse's face, and sank down into the same chair she had occupied earlier in the day.

'Harry? Are you here too?'

'Yes, Grandma.'

The voice from the bed grew stronger, more positive, and for the first time Stacey could see and hear the dominant force of this pioneer woman. 'Harry, you take yourself and that nice little nurse, and go talk to your horses, or something. I want to talk to Kitten alone.'

He grinned down at Stacey, his face cast in shadows by the tiny light, then shrugged his shoulders. 'So OK,' he said softly, 'Nurse and I are going. For fifteen minutes, not a second longer.'

'Git!' the old lady snapped at him. But there was a smile on her tired face too. 'Now, girl.' She fumbled on top of the coverlet until Stacey put her hand in the way. It was snatched up in a death-grip.

'You were gone a long time, Kitten. I'd almost given up.' There was a silence which Stacey felt driven to fill.

'I—I had to have time to think,' she said sweetly. 'Everybody was pushing at me to—'

'I know, girl—To marry Harry. That was all my fault. But now you've done it, you must work to make him happy. He's overworked, supporting us all. Promise?'

'I—' Stacey stopped in mid-sentence. Pushing me to marry Harry? Just the way Aunt Ellen was pushing me to marry George? Is that the way it always happens? Have I been wrong all this time, to think I was the only one treated like that? But then how much pushing would it have taken for them to get me to marry Harry!

'He's a good man,' the voice from the bed whispered. 'We all lean on him, and he has nobody to help him.' The old lady's strength was fading. Her eyes were half closed, and she was breathing rapidly.

Stacey squeezed her hand gently. 'I promise,' she said, 'For all my life.'

There was a sigh of contentment, then suddenly the hand in hers went limp. Stacey bent over the bed anxiously, but the old woman was still breathing. Lying still, with a smile on her face, but still breathing. Stacey fell back into the chair again, clinging to the fragile hand, repeating all she could remember of the prayers she had learned in the Lutheran Church near her home. The nurse came back silently, after a full half-hour, and looked carefully at her patient.

'She won't wake up again until morning,' she whispered. 'You might as well get some sleep.'

Harry was waiting for her, outside in the hall. 'We've got a small problem,' he said lightly as he led her in the other direction, around the stairs, and into a separate wing. Things were different on this side of the house. All the window curtains were drawn back, room doors were open, and brilliant lighting banished the dark memories of the wing behind them. As usual, he was going full speed, towing her behind him by her wrist.

'What small problem?' she gasped. 'And could you slow down?'

'Oh!' He came to a full stop, with his hand on the knob of the only closed door in the wing. 'You'll have to keep reminding me,' he said. 'You're tall for a girl, and I forget about short legs.'

'It isn't the legs, it's my skirt,' she snapped at him. He opened the door and almost pushed her into the room.

'I somehow knew there was nothing wrong with your legs,' he leered. 'That's the first thing I noticed on the plane.'

'Stop drooling,' she snapped, irritated. 'Just tell me what the problem is.' But instead of telling her he showed her, with a wide sweeping gesture. The bedroom was as large as three of her own, back at the ranch. The décor was gold and white—a woman's room, without a doubt. Three delicate chairs were scattered around a large queen-sized bed, which held pride of position between two bay windows. On a small coffee table at the foot of the bed there were three suitcases, two of Harry's, and one of hers. Suddenly she felt a chill.

She looked up at him. He frowned down at her and shrugged his shoulders. 'Servants,' he said dolefully. 'When you grow up with them, they tend to dictate. This is the only room prepared.'

'I don't think I'm going to like what you're going to tell me,' Stacey said determinedly. 'We're going to share a room?'

'Well, almost,' he sighed. 'Not actually, but we have to give Millie that impression, otherwise there's bound to be some hint of it given to Grandmother.'

'So?' She was trembling again, but not from any emotion she had ever experienced before. There was something about this whole affair that gave it the aura of *déjà vu*. Or perhaps It was something out of an old Hollywood 'B' picture. In any case, she intended to be on her guard, and give him no advantages.

'So we have to make this room look lived in,' he sighed, 'even though I'm going to sneak down the hall for the night. Right?'

'That all depends,' she said cautiously.

'On what?'

'Oh how much "living in" we're expected to provide,' she snapped. 'I'm going to bed. You'd better do your act and get down the hall.'

'You bet,' he said. He was wearing a big smile, a big artificial smile. 'The bathroom's there to your right.'

With the door locked behind her, Stacey languished in the hot water, using somebody else's bubble bath, and splashing herself liberally with lotion afterwards. Her bag contained only one nightgown, an old cotton ankle-length that she had worn for three years, and had almost outgrown, especially around several interesting places.

Sure that Harry would be a long time, she strolled out into the bedroom again, scuffing her feet in the softness of the thick pile rug. The bedroom lights were off, but there was enough starlight stealing in through the double windows to outline the bed. She hummed as she walked over to it, pulled back the corner of the sheets, and slipped into the softness, the blessed softness. Her bed at home felt like a board. This one sank and rose to meet every curve. She lay down flat on her back, and stretched both arms sidewise, in the sheer joy of it all. The contentment lasted just long enough for the nerves in her left hand to report that somebody else was sharing the bed with her!

She sat up, clutching at the sheets, tensed to scream, when Harry's big hand sealed her mouth. She struggled against him, but the weight of the sheets entangled her. 'Hey,' he said, 'I told you it has to look real!'

She broke away from his grip, and managed to get her feet on the floor. 'It doesn't have to look *this* real,' she snapped at him. 'What the devil do you think you're doing!'

'I'm just setting the scene,' he retorted. 'My God, why did I have to get a *child* for this!' The comment stung. A child—Lord, she was tired of that classification! She was a long way from being a child, damn him. I'll show him *child*! She sat back, pulled her feet back under the sheets, and stretched out again.

'Okay,' she snapped at him, 'what's the next act?'

'Well, we have to squirm around, get close, dent the pillows, and everything like that.'

'And then you go down the hall?'

'Yup.'

'Okay, start squirming.' That last sentence ended in a squeak, as he squirmed up close against her, dropping one hand across her stomach. 'Now it's your turn,' he whispered in her ear.

'My turn to what?'

'Squirm,' he chuckled. 'Wriggle closer. Put your arms around me.'

Stacey bit her lip. 'You'd better be sure it's all necessary,' she hissed at him, but he made no answer. So squirm, she told herself. She turned towards him, feeling the warmth of bare skin brushing against her barely covered breasts. She gasped at the shock, and almost drew back, but his encircling arms held her close. Gradually she extended a finger in his direction, and it bounced off his hip. Nothing but skin, her sensors reported.

Oh Lord, what do I do next? she asked herself. Nothing she had ever learned had prepared her for this. His arms locked her in—and strangely enough, she was enjoying it! She moved slightly, the change brushing her aroused breasts against the solid warmth of his chest. He lay very quietly. Asleep? She held her breath, trying to monitor his. He was inhaling deeply, just the tiniest bit noisily.

Why, damn the man, he's gone to sleep, she told herself bitterly. He really *does* think of me as a child. Listen to him! But her fractious body was paying no attention. One of her hands came back to his hip, traced a careful line upward, across his narrow waist, up on to his muscular chest, and farther, up into his hair. He stirred slightly, but settled again.

The length and tenor of her day began to catch up to her. It's warm here, she sighed to herself. Warm, and comfortable—nice. And what harm can he do if he's asleep? She snuggled even closer. Her eyelids grew too heavy, and she dropped off to sleep.

When he was sure she was asleep he moved carefully on to his back, a broad grin on his face, and pulled her head into a more comfortable position on his shoulder. Man, have you got willpower! he told himself. His hand moved slowly downward to cup her breast. That's enough, his conscience dictated. Lord, is this *child* loaded! His hand moved gently down to rest on the swell of her hip, and there he managed to rein himself in. Some time later he too fell asleep.

They were both awakened by a knock on the door, and Millie Fallon came in, not waiting for an invitation, and not at all abashed by seeing them so close together. The sun was coming in the windows, bright with the promise of a new day. The early morning birds were hard at work, and a slight breeze flavoured the room. 'The doctor's been,' Millie announced. 'I thought you'd like to hear first hand.'

She beckoned, and an elderly white-haired man came into the bedroom. Oh, my God, groaned Stacey as she ducked her head under the covers. It's not enough to be caught in his bed, but the darn place is like a train depot!

Harry sat up in the bed, reading Stacey's mind. Under the covers his big hand came down on her well-padded bottom, and gave an admonitory whack. 'Doctor Jenkins,' he acknowledged. 'What is it?'

'The nurse called me a couple of hours ago,' the doctor replied. 'Your grandmother has slipped into a coma. It might last a day, or a week—maybe even longer. But I think you have to accept the fact that she will never wake up. And I've got to run. The nurse has my instructions.'

Mrs Fallon shooed him out of the room, turning back in the doorway before she closed it. 'And you two better have some breakfast. Downstairs in twenty minutes.' The housekeeper sniffed a couple of times at the tear breaking from her right eye, and went off.

Stacey poked her head timidly out from beneath the covers. 'I thought you were supposed to go down the hall,' she snapped.

'I seem to have fallen asleep,' Harry returned innocently. 'I hope it didn't inconvenience you?'

'No—no, not at all,' she stammered. Not for the life of her was she going to tell him that she had wakened at three in the morning, and found his hand on the peak of her breast, driving her into emotions she had not ever thought about before. It had been bad enough to feel that nervous shiver that came when her pills were late. But to have—this—on top of it? Not for the life of her would she tell him!

CHAPTER THREE

It was nine o'clock on Monday morning when the big car came out of Gatesville, and turned south on Highway 116, in the direction of Pidcoke. 'It's about a mile south from here,' Stacey directed from her corner, close against the door of the car, and as far as she could get from Harry without actually getting out. 'There's a little sigh, and a dirt road: Rancho Miraflores. Dad was stationed in the Canal Zone, you know.'

He grunted an answer. His humour hadn't improved since Saturday morning, she told herself. That was the moment he had received the news of his grandmother's aggravated problem, and from then on he had plunged into a round of notifications and instructions, while Stacey had done her level best to keep out of his way. Far out of his way. Waking up in the morning, finding him next to her in bed, not wearing a stitch, had blown her eighteen-year-old mind. Sunday's meals had been catch as catch can. And then, on Sunday night, he had tracked her down on the veranda.

'We'll leave tomorrow—early,' he told her. He sounded tired—and no wonder. The doctor had called twice, with worse news each time. There was no hope for his grandmother. 'Tomorrow some time, my Aunt Angela is coming,' he added. 'I want to get you settled before then.'

Translate that to, 'I want to get you out of here before she smells a rat,' Stacey told herself. He's too proud to have me meet his aunt. Is it me, or is it his family? Me, probably. Why would he want to unload a troubled teenager on his family, at a time like this? So he'll whisk me home to Aunt Ellen, and run. And I can't blame him, can I? If I helped his grandmother at all, it was because she deserved it, nothing else. And if he stayed in my bed all night—well, nothing really happened. Did it? That was the question that had bothered her all during the fifty-mile drive from his home to the gates of Rancho Miraflores.

She could feel her own disappointment, after weekending at Rosedale, his grandmother's home. The ranch house was an unpainted wooden structure, all on one floor, with two weatherbeaten wings sheltering ten rooms and only one bath. It had been great for herself and her father. But now—she sighed, and knew that he saw with a rancher's eyes the dried-up land stretching to the horizon, the battered barbed wire fences, the empty barns. Despite the fact that the pumps could be seen in the distance, nodding their heads over black gold, the house looked as if it hadn't seen a penny of repairs for years. And the open range land, even close to the house, barely held down by a smattering of rough grass, looked promising grounds for high winds to strip.

'It's not much,' she offered in apology.

'All it needs is work,' he returned. 'Work and money, and a little water. There should be underground water in these parts; there are all kinds of creeks in the area, and the Lampassas River isn't too far away. Is that your Aunt?'

Stacey looked up at the house, to where Aunt Ellen was standing on the porch. 'Yes,' she sighed, then hesitated as Harry came around to open her door. The early morning heat smashed at her as the car's air-conditioning died. It was the kind of day depicted in the old Texas joke, where the hawk chased the pigeon, both carrying their lunch, and both walking. She struggled out of the seat and forced her feet to function.

Block your ears, she told herself, as she mounted the two steps to the porch. The first blast from the Delanos will knock you back to Gatesville, and the second will probably take you all the way out of Coryelle County. But, surprisingly, there was no blast at all. When she

reached the door her aunt was standing there, slightly
slumped, her shoulders bent, and tears rolling down her
face.

'Aunt Ellen?' she queried.

'They're gone, Stacey. Packed up and gone.'

'You mean Uncle Henry?'

'Yes. What did you say to him? What, Stacey?'

'She said nothing. I said a great deal,' Harry interjected. 'Are we going to discuss it on the porch?'

'Come in,' invited Stacey, and her aunt looked up,
shocked. 'It's *my* house,' Stacey said coldly. 'It took me
a long time to realise that, but it's my house. Come in,
Harry.'

The other two followed her into the living room.
Looking with newly opened eyes, she could see that it
was a tacky room—old furniture, falling to pieces in
places, a worn rug, and dirty curtains at the windows.
Harry looked around searchingly, but made no comment. He took the biggest chair, without invitation. Her
aunt sat stiffly on the edge of one of the rickety straight
chairs.

'And you're the one? Stacey's husband?' There was a
trace of defiance in Aunt Ellen's voice, but only a trace.

'Yes, I'm the one,' he said. 'Stacey, could you get me a
cup of coffee while I talk to your aunt?'

'I—I'd rather—' I'd rather stay and listen, she meant
to say, but his eyebrows went up, and there was that
imperious look on his face, so she retreated into the
kitchen. But no amount of looking down Harry's nose
would make her close the door behind her. She started
on the coffee makings automatically, with an ear glued
to the living room. Her hand trembled as she measured
the coffee into the pot.

'Now first,' he said, 'we'll get rid of this idea of yours
that you're Stacey's guardian. She's of age, according to
Texas law, and you have no powers over her.'

'But she gave me her power of attorney—signed
legally, and all.'

'Tear it up,' he snorted. 'Since she married after the event, the paper isn't worth a penny. This morning she executed another power of attorney, superseding yours, and naming me. As her husband I have certain other legal rights. Among them, Mrs Delano, is the right to call for an accounting. Where are her property records for the last two years?'

'Henry—he burned them all last night. And—oh God—the strongbox!' exclaimed Aunt Ellen.

'What about the strongbox?'

'We've been cashing the quarterly oil lease payments, and putting the money in the strongbox. Henry said it was best, in these times, to have the ready cash, rather than tie it all up in a bank vault.'

'I'll bet he did,' said Harry sarcastically. 'Where is it?'

'In his study. I'll—it will only take a minute.'

'You bet,' Harry said again. 'I'll come with you.' Their voices faded into the distance, and Stacey shook her head in disgust. Just at the interesting part! That's always the way when you're snooping, she thought. She reached up to the third shelf for cups, and as she stretched to her limits her hands began to shake, and a pain struck in her stomach. Nausea followed, leaving a feeling of weakness and disorientation. The cups in her hands fell to the floor, and in a moment she followed.

When she came to she was lying on the couch in the living room, her head on Harry's lap, while tender hands smoothed her brow with a cold wet cloth. 'What happened?' he demanded.

'I—I don't know,' she stammered. Her voice was slurred, and her head ached, but her stomach had settled down. 'I was reaching for some cups, and I felt sick, and then everything—I just don't know.' His heavy hand rested on her forehead, quieting some of the trembling that was still shaking her.

'I don't think you've got a fever,' he started to say, and looked across at her aunt. The older woman had never been one to hide her feelings, and now running across her disfigured face was a guilty look.

'You've seen this before, Mrs Delano?' His voice was cold enough to freeze a side of beef. Aunt Ellen shook her head and reached into the pocket of her dress for a handkerchief. When she pulled it out a plastic container of pills came with it, and rolled out into the middle of the floor. Harry was on it before the older woman could make a move.

'My God!' he roared. 'Is this what you've been feeding the child? Valium? What doctor prescribed this?'

'No doctor.' Aunt Ellen was crying. 'Henry got them—he has friends in Dallas. The girl gets excitable, and we had to calm her down.'

'Yes, I'll bet you did.' His tongue dripped bitter venom, enough to send Aunt Ellen out of her chair, shrinking back against the windowsill. 'And how long have you been feeding her this stuff?'

'Two—two years.'

'No wonder she's sick!—a perfect case of withdrawal symptoms. Damn you all! Where's the telephone!'

At this point Stacey closed her eyes. She could hear words, endless words. She felt someone pick her up, carry her to her room, undress her, and tuck her in. But beyond that, nothing really penetrated. The voices continued in the distance—roars, followed by weeping. And then in succession, separate cars arriving at the door, and finally the roar of a helicopter.

Shortly after that she could feel cold hands exploring her body, the touch of metal at her chest and back, a peering into her eyes, the slight pain of a hypodermic needle. Then things quieted down, and she slept.

Harry was sitting by her bed when she woke up. Her mouth tasted furry, and her vision was slightly blurred, but her stomach had settled. She smiled weakly up at him. 'I seem to be a continual problem to you, don't I?' she asked.

He moved over to the bed and looked down at her.

Searching for something, her mind told her. 'I brought my own doctor in from Waco,' he said. 'He says you're going through withdrawal symptoms, a sort of Valium poisoning. He gave you a couple of shots—a sedative, and some B12 vitamins.'

'What do I do now?'

'It depends on how tough you are, Kitten—I mean Stacey. Can you take it straight?'

'I—I don't know, do I? I guess I can. Take what straight?'

'If you think you can take it, love, it's like kicking a barbiturate habit cold turkey. All you have to do is stick it out for a couple of weeks, then you're home free.'

'Otherwise?' she asked.

'Otherwise is four to six weeks in a hospital facility, while they wean you from it all. Your choice.'

'I—I'll take it straight,' she sighed. 'I'm really not all that brave, but I would rather try.'

'That's my girl! Your best bet is to keep your mind occupied and your stomach empty—relatively, that is.'

Stacey watched him, fighting a touch of nausea at the same time. He looked—just a tiny bit more handsome than when she had first seen him. He was never really ugly, she told herself, and now—why, now he's almost handsome! 'What else has happened?' she asked.

'Not much.' He sat down on the edge of the bed and picked up one of her hands, treasuring it against his cheek to help her control the trembling. The way your husband would, her conscience reminded her. As if— but of course, he couldn't; that would be silly. She tried her best to wipe the wistfulness from her face.

'First of all,' he said, 'you mustn't take it too seriously, but as best I can figure out, you're broke. Your Uncle Henry made off with all the money in the strongbox, and we don't even know how much that is. I called Parsons Oil, and they'll reconstruct your income account for you. At least that way you'll know how much he stole from you.'

She laughed up at him. 'You're fooling me, Harry. I've called Parsons a time or two myself, and they won't tell anybody anything. Do you expect me to believe that you just picked up the telephone and—'

'I'm darned if that wasn't just what I did,' Harry said solemnly. 'They must have mistaken me for somebody else, because I got instant service. How about that!'

'Well—' she was still suspicious, 'I suppose it could have been an accident. And then what?'

'And then I called the Texas Rangers. Your uncle is being charged with embezzlement, and other crimes. I also have a lawyer who's looking into this business about him prescribing medicines without a licence, and things like that.'

'Oh, wow!' she giggled. 'I don't suppose you could think of some reason for arresting George too?'

'I haven't come to that yet,' he chuckled. 'How about for proposing marriage in bad faith? If I could get him into court and show he's afraid of horses, any jury in Texas would put him away for life.'

'And Aunt Ellen?'

'That's not for me to say, Stacey. You have to decide. She's a very shaken lady, with no place to go. Do you want her arrested?'

'Lord no, Harry! Before Delano came she was good to me. I can't have my father's only sister arrested. Leave her here with me.'

He smiled and nodded agreement. Why, he's a wonderful man, she thought. Won't he just make some lucky girl a fine husband! 'I suppose you'll have to go back,' she offered hesitantly.

'In a day or so,' he said gruffly. 'I'm bringing in a staff of nurses, and a temporary housekeeper for you, but until then, I mean to stick it out here. Okay?'

But in the event, he didn't go in a day or so. He stayed on, spending the whole of that first night comforting her, rushing her to the bathroom when nausea overcame her, changing her nightgown twice, and sponging her down.

And when the nurses arrived the next day, he continued waiting on her through those miserable days, when she was too sick to eat, and yet dared not stop, for fear of the pain of the empty stomach. The doctor came twice, with more vitamin shots and considerable sympathy.

For more than a week she was a very sick girl, and he remained at her side, doing everything necessary, until she began to realise that nobody in the world knew her body as well as he did. He seemed—almost—to really be a husband to her. And when she was finally allowed out of her bedroom it seemed only proper that they would breakfast together in the kitchen, she in her robe, drinking her tea, and he reading the morning paper in his shirt sleeves.

She established a shambling sort of peace with Aunt Ellen, too—an aunt who was dogged by a guilty conscience, and was trying her best to make up for it.

At the end of the second week Stacey walked out around the ranch buildings with Harry, happy to see that someone had been taking care of her old quarter horse, Ramona. 'You could ride her if you please,' she offered, remembering that he had talked about daily rides for exercise.

'Me?' he laughed. 'On that critter? What is she, ten—twelve hands high? I hate to ride a horse that's smaller than me.'

It tickled her fancy, and she giggled. 'Well, Ramona needs the exercise as much as you do,' she chortled. 'Why don't you let her ride you?'

It was said in all innocence, but Harry retaliated by chasing her around the outside of the stable, her steps wobbly but firm, until she collapsed in a bundle of laughter by the old hand pump that stood in the yard.

He came up behind her, puffing a little, and swept her up in his arms. 'You're a sparky little kid, aren't you?' he panted. 'Two more laps and I could have had a stroke or something!' His face was just a few inches from hers, his mouth wide, displaying a forest of straight white teeth. Close enough to—but whatever she had been about to say was squeezed out of her as he moved her an inch or two in his arms, and her full strong breasts scraped across his chest, where only his thin cotton shirt and her even thinner blouse separated them. Harry drew in his breath with a hiss, and Stacey was so started by the impact that she hardly knew what to do next. I hope he'll kiss me, she told herself. But he didn't.

He stared down at her, then gently put her down on her feet. Still holding her close, he tilted up her chin with his index finger, and concentrated on her eyes. 'Whatever made me think you're a kid?' he half whispered. 'Don't you ever wear a bra?'

She dropped her eyes and let her hair swing over her face. His hands flexed on her arms, then released her. She stepped back away from him, leaving the question unanswered. 'I think we'd better go in,' he finally managed. 'All this might be too much for you.'

There was no room for argument. He took her by the arm and hurried her across the desolate back yard and into the house, where he turned her over to her aunt, and disappeared into his bedroom.

The house was quiet that night. The nurses had been released—happy to go, apparently, since Harry did all the work. And the temporary housekeeper was packing her bags for an early departure in the morning. When he came down to dinner he was a different man, cool, detached, almost as if he had put all the adventures behind him. He made three telephone calls, then came in for the meal.

'I'll bring you up to date,' he told Stacey, as the soup came in. 'The Rangers have an all-points bulletin out on the Delanos, and the County Sheriff has agreed to have a patrol keep a good watch on the house for the next few days.'

Stacey could not meet his eyes. With her attention focused on the soup plate, she spooned at it, and nodded her head, hoping that he would not see the growing despair on her face.

'I've also made arrangements with Parsons Oil,' he went on, while Aunt Ellen brought in the steak. Like an armoured assault column, Stacey told herself. He knows I don't want to hear, but he's going to tell me—for my own good, I suppose. He doesn't seem to realise that 'my own good' has changed—changed drastically. It's only been three weeks since I met him for the first time, and everything has changed. But he doesn't care. Look at him!

'They'll make your next quarterly payment in advance, two weeks from today. The cheque will go directly to an account in the First National Bank of Waco, and half will be put in a checking account, the other half into an investment fund. You can begin drawing on it on the eighteenth.'

'I—I suppose it would be graceless to ask how much?' she managed to get out.

'Not at all. Your quarterly payment comes to seventy-six thousand dollars.'

Her spoon clattered as it hit the edge of her plate and bounced on the floor. Across the table from her, Aunt Ellen began to cry, soft soundless tears, that dripped across the huge disfiguring birthmark on her face and dropped into her coffee cup.

At eight o'clock that evening, in the last of a lingering twilight, they heard the roar of the helicopter. It landed in the flat area between the house and the stable. Harry came into the kitchen, where Stacey was hiding—to be truthful about it—and led her out of the house, bag in one hand, she on the other. Halfway between the flying machine and the house he dropped the bag and pulled her around to face him.

'I didn't want your aunt to hear,' he said. 'It's been a wonderful couple of weeks, Stacey, very different from my ordinary routine. And now I have to go. I thank you from the bottom of my heart for what you did for my grandmother. It meant more than I can say. And it's been a lot of fun, having such a lovely young wife. Some day you're going to meet a man who will welcome you as his *real* wife. And I'll read about it in the papers, and envy him every bit of his good luck. Goodbye, Kitten.'

Stacey struggled to keep a smile on her face, despite the fact that her heart was breaking into tiny little pieces. Yes, I'll make somebody a fine wife, she wanted to shout at him, but dared not. I'd make *you* a fine wife. And you wouldn't even have to ask. Just give me one small sign that you want me. Just one small sign! Or—if you don't want a wife—if you would just say, and I'd come with you, right now. The words were close on her lips, and slipped out. 'Do you need a mistress?'

She clutched herself close up against his chest, so he would not see the burning flash of shame that crossed her expressive face. What could a man say to something like that!

'No,' he said gently, 'I don't need a mistress. And you don't need some casual lover, Stacey Bronfield. Go back to the house and give this whole crazy mix-up some thought. I'm much too old for you, little lady. Some day a man will come for you, never fear.'

She backed away from him, into the gathering darkness. Some day a man will come for me? she thought. If he does, he'll find a girl who has already been spoiled, ruined by memories. She wanted to run screaming after him. You're not too old for me, she wanted to shout. I may be too young, but it's something I'll grow out of, if you'll just give me time!

In the vague twilight of sub-tropical Texas his figure wavered as he moved towards the helicopter. The door slammed, the engine reverberated across the empty farmland, and he was gone, transformed from a lean, loving man to a pair of blinking lights in the sky, gradually fading away.

Stacey went back into the house, her face locked in the stiff control she had clamped over it outside. But once inside her bedroom her control failed, and she fell on to her bed, face down, burying her grief in her pillows, so her aunt would not be alarmed by the wailing.

A sort of mutual gloom settled over the house for the next few days. The temporary housekeeper had gone, and Aunt Ellen reigned in kitchen and in house. And gradually, as they both realised that there was no one else to turn to, she and Stacey turned to each other. Small talk, at first, then brief confidences that led, over the days, to a mutual respect which had never existed before.

Stacey spent most of her mornings riding over the ranch, exploring the places she had known as a little girl, the places that had disappeared from her drug-shrouded memory in these latter years. Afternoons she devoted to housework, draining her aunt's mind of those myriad little things that go into making a house run smoothly. And there were countless hours in the kitchen, where Stacey quickly learned those skills which her aunt had long hidden. Stacey had a goal, even though she did not know how to achieve it.

Two weeks after Harry had left Aunt Ellen finally broke down. When Stacey came in from her lonely ride, she found the older woman bent over the kitchen table, crying her heart out. A picture of Uncle Henry lay in the middle of the table. Much wiser in the ways of the world than she had been four weeks before, Stacey offered comfort, but made no effort to shut off the tears. After a good hour of lamenting, her aunt was ready to talk. Stacey made instant coffee, and waited. Somehow, she knew, she must get the older woman talking. A great catharsis, talking; the American woman's escape from reality. The home psychiatrist, so to speak. And it worked.

'I knew it would come one day,' her aunt mused. 'I knew it from the very beginning, but I just took one day at a time, and tried to avoid all the tomorrows.'

'He loved you?' queried Stacey.

'Love had something to do with it, but it wasn't love of me. He fell in love with the ranch, first thing out of the barrel. But I guess it was only fair. I didn't love him, either.'

'I don't understand. Why did you marry him if you didn't love him?'

'You don't understand, Stacey. You're young, and all the world is beautiful—and so are you. But I'm not. Life has passed me by already. I had none of the things that other women have and want—a home, children, love. I wanted it all, and love just really didn't rank at the top.' Her light voice held bitterness in its cup, bitterness that overflowed and flavoured her whole life.

'For a beautiful girl like you, Stacey, there's always a beautiful man waiting. For women like me—her hand unconsciously brushed across her disfigured cheek, 'for women like me, there just isn't much available. You have to play the hand God dealt you. Henry wasn't much—I knew that the day I met him, and he never proved me wrong. But he was a man, and I was his wife. There was that feeling—that feeling of belonging. Belonging—that's what it's all about, isn't it?'

Stacey looked down at the bowed grey head, and understanding came. She leaned forward over the table and ran her fingers through the iron-grey hair. 'It's all right,' she whispered. 'I understand. We still have each other.'

The next day started off in a companionable warmth between the two surviving members of the Bronfield clan. But it lasted hardly until ten o'clock, when a sheriff's car pulled up in the yard, and heavy boots climbed up the front stairs.

He was a big man, perhaps a little too old for his job, with forty excess pounds around his belly. But the badge was official, and the paper he presented was legal enough to shake Stacey in her boots.

After she had invited him into the living room he

doffed his ten-gallon hat, made uncomfortable noises, then came right to the point. 'I'm serving papers for the County Tax office,' he explained, as he handed her a triple-fold sheet of paper.

'What's this?' she asked in amazement.

'You *are* Stacey Bronfield, the owner of this spread, aren't you?'

She nodded, not able to summon the proper words. Aunt Ellen came into the room at the same time, and stood absolutely still. 'I still don't understand,' muttered Stacey at the Sheriff's officer.

'Taxes,' he explained. 'You haven't paid the taxes on this place for the past four years. The county is preparing to take court action to foreclose unless these taxes are paid in the next forty-eight hours.'

'Forty-eight hours?' Her mind was moving desperately. It was still another week before payments from the oil company would be paid, and as of that moment she was totally broke. Harry had left two hundred dollars behind. 'A feed stake,' he had said. 'Enough to keep you eating until the royalties come in.' But two hundred dollars was hardly enough for—or was it?

'How much do I owe?' she asked timidly.

The Sheriff's officer looked down at the paper, still in his hand. 'It says here, payments and interest included, twenty-two thousand dollars, ma'am. Land is still pretty valuable.'

Stacey could feel the ground shake under her feet. Where in the world was she going to get that kind of money? Poor little rich girl! Hundreds of gallons of oil were being pumped out of her land every day, and she hadn't the money to pay the tax bill. She looked across at her aunt, the anguish showing on her face. 'And I only have forty-eight hours to pay it up?'

'That's what the judge said, ma'am. Forty-eight hours, or the county forecloses for taxes.'

'And then what?'

'And then they auction the spread, and apply what

they get to the tax bill. If there's anything left over, you get it. Although from the looks of the place, you'll be lucky to break even. Don't you have any friends you could call?'

'That's it,' Aunt Ellen shrieked in her ear. 'Call him!'

Still in a daze, Stacey just could not comprehend. 'Call who?'

'Why, your husband, of course!'

'Your husband?' The Sheriff's officer began to smile. It made a difference. Coming ten miles to foreclose a place on two women was not his idea of a fun thing. But if there was a husband—well, that was a different breed of cat. 'By all means call your husband,' he offered.

'But I—he'll be working,' stammered Stacey. 'And I don't know—I don't have his number, and—'

'He left his card,' said Aunt Ellen. She was already at the telephone, dialling, 'before he went off. He left his card with me and said I was to call if anything went wrong. And what better than this? Hello? Yes, I want to speak to Mr Marsden, please. Who's calling? His wife, of course. Stacey, what is that idiotic name he calls you? No, operator, his secretary won't do. I need Mr Marsden. His wife is in a lot of trouble, and—don't you dare talk to me like that!'

'Let me take it,' Stacey intervened. There was a cool secretarial voice on the other end. 'And Mr Marsden is definitely not married,' it said.

Stacey's dander was up—a compound of foreclosure notices, supercilious secretaries, and a vast need to pound somebody in the mouth. 'A lot you know,' she snapped down the line. 'Please tell Harry that Kitten is on the line. And do it quickly!'

It was her tone of voice, rather than the words, that brought attention. She could hear keys click at the other end, and eventually that deep familiar voice. It cheered her, and all her anger drained out of her.

'Well? Who is it?' he roared.

'It's me,' she said very weakly. 'If you remember—'

'Kitten?'

'Yes, it's me.'

'Why the devil didn't you say so! I'm in the middle of a big meeting. Can't it wait?'

It was hard to keep the tears out of her voice. Lord, he was angry! She fumbled for excusing words. 'I—I'm sure it can wait,' she cried, 'but if it does they're going to foreclose on the ranch and take everything because we didn't pay the taxes for the last four years and the Sheriff is here—no, that's wrong. He says he's only a Deputy Sheriff. But he's here with a paper from the judge and he says if we don't pay twenty-two thousand dollars he— what? Oh. And twenty-six cents, he's going to seize the property and sell it all at auction or something, and I've only got forty-eight hours to get—what did you say?'

'I said stop!' Harry yelled down the line. 'Stop and take a deep breath. Take two deep breaths. Come on, let me hear them.' Stacey struggled to master her confusion, breathing deeply, clenching her teeth to keep them from rattling.

'All right now,' he said softly. 'Follow along. A Deputy Sheriff is there. Right?' She nodded. 'Right?' he repeated. She nodded again, half paralysed by his anger.

'He can't hear you shake your head,' the Deputy suggested. This stop was about to make his day. He had looked forward to a gloomy time, serving four foreclosure notices, and here at the second stop there was entertainment galore.

'No,' Stacey stammered, 'of course he can't.'

'What did you say?' the voice at the other end asked.

'I said no, you can't hear me when I shake my head.'

She could hear the rattle of his sigh as it came down the wire and reverberated in her ear. 'Please—please don't be mad,' she begged.

'I'm not, Kitten.' His voice still had that soft low caress. 'Let's do it again. The Deputy Sheriff is there with a tax notice, and he wants twenty-two thousand dollars for—'

'And twenty-six cents,' she interrupted.

'Yes, and twenty-six cents. Or else he's going to foreclose on the ranch. Have I got that right?'

'Yes,' she mumbled. 'But I suppose it can wait. I really don't want to bother you, and I wouldn't have, but Aunt Ellen—'

'Oh, shut up,' he snapped. 'I thank the Lord for your aunt. Now, listen closely.'

'Yes, sir?'

'Don't *sir* me, damnit! Just listen. Go make the nice man a cup of coffee, and smile at him a lot. I'll be there in thirty minutes.'

'Thirty minutes? How can you do that? Where are you?'

'I'm in Waco,' he chuckled, 'and there's a helicopter on the pad outside. If you'll only stop talking and start moving I'll be on my way. Now what do you have to say?'

'Goodbye? Sir?'

'I'll get you for that!' he snapped, but the threatening tone was missing.

Stacey turned to the Deputy and tried a smile. It was a second-hand sort of smile, but it served its purpose. The big officer, content that a man was coming to talk to him, settled back in the chair next to the window, and was prepared to be entertained.

Harry was wrong, of course. It took him twenty-five minutes, the flight being the easiest part of it. When the helicopter boosted to one thousand feet and moved north to skirt the restricted area around Fort Hood, he was still laying down the law to his accountant about money. And his lawyer, who was supposed to have checked for this sort of thing beforehand.

So he stomped into the house at just a peg below tornado force, and began to express certain strong opinions before the door closed behind him. Stacey dived for her bedroom and slammed her door behind her. She could still hear him giving directions out in the living room. Her eyes searched frantically for some way to bar the door. She pushed with all her might, trying to move the lowboy up against the door panels, but Harry pushed the door, the lowboy, and herself aside as he burst in without knocking.

She stood stock still in the middle of the room, head up, shoulders back. I'll go down fighting, she told herself. Lord, is he angry! His face is all red!

'Come here,' he commanded, and all her resolve about going down fighting flew immediately out the window. She took one hesitant step in his direction, then ran the rest of the way, hurling herself into his welcome arms. When he kissed her through all the tears, it was like a reprieve from a life sentence. One touch and he brought comfort. His mouth roamed down her neck, and nibbled at her ear lobe—and back up.

The second touch on her half-opened lips blew the top of her skull off, and left her desperately striving to hold on around his neck. The floor rocked, tensions disappeared. She pressed into him until her feet came off the floor. She was panting when he set her down again. And he was no model of calm concern, either; it did her composure a great deal of good to see that he was shaken, perhaps almost as much as she.

'Good God,' he muttered, 'I didn't realise marriage was all this tough. What ever in the world am I going to do with you?'

'Pay my taxes?' she offered wistfully.

'What? Is that all you can think of?' he laughed. 'One kiss and I pay your taxes? Well, I've got two people out in the other room taking care of that little problem. But what am I going to do about you?'

'I'm growing older terribly fast,' Stacey offered hesitantly. 'I think I've aged five years in the past five hours. Perhaps you could—'

'Perhaps I could what?'

Love me? she whispered under her breath. But Harry had already turned away to give instructions to the other two men, and apparently missed her comment.

He stayed for lunch. The other two, his lawyer and his accountant, went into Gatesville with the Deputy Sheriff, 'to make sure there are no more loose ends,' he told her.

After the meal they sat out in front on the worn porch swing, watching a flock of crows squabbling over something in the pasture. They sat comfortably close, close enough for thighs to touch, and for his hand to drape naturally over her shoulder.

'So I guess I must have made a little mistake,' he said.

'I can't imagine what you mean,' Stacey returned idly. 'I never conceive of the Harry Marsdens of this world making mistakes, big or little.'

'Hey! A little sarcasm there,' he chuckled. 'You *are* growing up in a hurry, aren't you?'

'Well,' she said meditatively, sticking her tongue out to gently moisten her dry lips, 'I'm not a very good judge of such things, but I *feel* older. In fact I feel like a wrung-out seventy-year-old woman right this minute. Does all that have some significance?'

'Hard to say. Look over there—two ducks flying east, a good luck sign. Make a wish.'

'I made one weeks ago,' she admitted shyly. 'I don't intend to make another until the first one comes true. Why did you say that about you'd made a little mistake?'

'Honest Injun?'

'Please.'

'Now, if you promise not to let this go to your head,' he began, 'I had a notion a time ago that you and I had done each other a favour, and were quits. So then, I thought, I'll just put this child out of my mind and—'

She stirred restlessly under his hand. 'Child?' she snapped.

'Well then, this young lady. Let me finish before I forget what I'm trying to say. What I meant was that I found it pretty hard to put this young lady out of my mind. Of course, the story of our marriage is all over Grandmother's property—and the neighbourhood.

And it leaked downtown into my office, too. And do you know something? It's added considerably to my stature, having a bride. So I thought—if you have no objection— that perhaps from time to time I might call on you for a little more bridal work, so to speak. If you don't object?'

Stacey did her best to keep from looking at him. Her face was too easily read, she was finding out, and the tear shadowing the corner of her eye was too much of a giveaway. She cleared her throat noisily. 'Sort of like Rent-a-Bride?' she suggested.

'Yes, sort of.' Harry sounded so serious that she had to look. His long craggy face was as solemn as a judge. The corners of his mouth were turned down, and he seemed poised—for a rejection. 'If you don't mind,' he repeated.

'No, I—I don't mind,' she said. The tinkling little laugh she had forced out to accompany words—to show him how casual she was about the whole idea—was so timid and so cold it even sent chills down *her* spine.

'Well, I think things are under control here,' he said coolly. 'And I've got a million things to do at work. By the way, Grandmother is still unchanged, in a coma. I'll keep you posted. And keep my telephone number close by, in case you need to rent a husband again. Right?'

Stacey couldn't get a word out in answer, so she sat stiffly on the edge of the swing and watched as he got up, stretched, and started around to the back of the house where the helicopter waited. Halfway down the path Harry stopped, hesitated, and came back.

'I'm not much up on this husband business,' he offered. 'I forgot this.' He leaned down and kissed her gently on the cheek, right over the spot where her dimple usually sparkled. And again, before she could get out a word, he wheeled around and left.

She was still sitting there rigidly when the roar of the engine announced his departure. Her left hand cupped her cheek where that goodbye salute had touched, and her right hand, on top of the other, twirled and fumbled at the two rings on her third finger, which she had never got around to removing.

CHAPTER FOUR

THE next few days seemed deadly dull. The sky clouded over, although no moisture fell to relieve the drought. Stacey began to ride again, saddling up early in the morning and wandering the far empty reaches of the ranch, where only the perpetually nodding pumps thumped back and forth, moving unseen oil up from the depths, forcing it into unseen pipes, and dispatching it to the Lord only knew where. Funny, she mused, as she dismounted beside one of the million No Trespassing signs, walked through the little gate marked Keep Out, and put her slender foot up on the wellhead cap. All that controlled movement going on beneath her feet, and only the lazy nodding head of the pump itself to indicate.

Wishing it were cattle instead of oil, she kicked at the cap, stubbed her toe, and continued miserably on her ride. She knew as well as anyone could, she told herself, that it wasn't the lack of cattle, or the broken-down fences, or the sere grazing land that made her ache. But I'm not going to think about *him*! she thought. Not at all. If he calls, well—maybe I might go to help him again. Maybe.

On Friday morning she came back to the house just before lunch, to find a gaggle of visitors. One group of three, surrounding an old drill-truck, looked somehow familiar. 'Steuben,' the elderly man introduced himself. 'My two boys.' He gestured at the two giants behind him, perhaps thirty-five to forty years old. 'We was over this way before your father—died. Water, he wanted, as I remember. I allus said they was water on this spread, you know, and your pa, he agreed with me.'

'I don't remember, Mr Steuben,' Stacey sighed. 'I

guess I was too young to think about it at the time.' She was finding it difficult to concentrate on the subject even now.

The other two men, lounging on the steps of the porch waiting their turn, were young—in their early twenties, perhaps, and dressed like working cattlemen.

'Well, I remember you, Stacey. Cutest little tyke, you was,' Mr Steuben continued. 'So I was sittin' to home the other day, business bein' slow like it is, and the telephone rings, and it's this girl from Waco. Mind you, I ain't got nothing agin Waco, there's nice folks over there, and all, but it done growed up from just a cattle town, and puts on airs, you know?'

She nodded. So many times she had listened to such conversations, at her father's side. There is just no hurrying a Texan when he's set in his ways, she thought. He'll talk it out eventually. She smiled at the old man, inviting more.

'Well, anyhow, turns out she's a secretary to some big shot in the city, and he comes on the line without no howdo-do or nothing. There's water on Rancho Miraflores, he says. And me, I ain't go no more idea in the world who he is, or what. So I says, is that true? And how do you know? And right quick he come back with, when they drilled the oil wells they found plenty water on the way down!'

Stacey's head shot up. If there was one thing she knew for sure, it was that wildcat oil drillers never, but never, ever told a soul about their drilling. Not ever!

'And?' she prompted.

'And to make a short story longer, as my pa used to say, we talks awhile about drillin', and he gives me a bunch of instructions. And when he hangs up I figure, well, that's the end of that. Some dude in the city pullin' my leg, or something. But the next day, here comes a Special Delivery, and it's got about six sections-charts, all from that Parsons Oil outfit, and they're marked for water. And attached on the front is this whoppin' big cheque—a certified cheque from the bank, mind you—all nice and pretty.'

'And that's it?'

'Nope. Underneath the cheque is a permit from Parsons Oil for me to drill anywheres on their leased land—for water. And then there was this note. Look here.' He reached into his overall pocket and pulled out a crumpled piece of paper. The heading on it said Marsden Management.

'Tell my wife,' the note said, 'that I want at least six bores put down.'

'And since I don't see no other young girls around, I guess you was her. His wife, I mean,' added Mr Steuben.

'Oh, I guess that's right,' muttered Stacey, not at all sure. 'I—well, what do you want me to say?'

'Not a word,' the old man laughed. 'We're supposed to begin close to the house, he said. And we'll start now. You just go about your business and don't pay us no mind, y'hear?' He waved at his two 'boys', who climbed on the truck without a word being spoken, and rattled around into the area behind the house. Their truck clattered and clanked as if on its last trip.

Stacey watched them, astonished. Water? It was all that was needed to make the land bloom. But who—or rather, why? And without even a word of explanation. How about that! You'd think we really *were* married, the way he gives long-distance orders around here! She backed up to the steps and sat down when she felt the pressure of the risers against her legs. 'I think I must be married to a dictator,' she said to nobody in particular.

'Seems as if.' One of the two young men lounging on the steps had spoken. She turned and glared at him—at them. Young, wiry, sun-creased faces. Cattlemen, and identical twins, for heaven's sake!

'All right,' she sighed, 'and just what the devil are you two doing here?'

'Can't rightly say,' the one closest to her announced. 'Morgan. I'm Jim and he's John.'

'Or maybe it's the other way around,' his twin commented.

'Heaven preserve me, a pair of comedians!' snapped Stacey. 'Let me start it off for you. You were sitting in your office and the telephone rang and it was—'

'No, ma'am,' Jim returned. 'Not like that at all. We work for Westland Cattle on their spread up the Brazos River. What with the drought and all, things have been tough. So the boss cornered us yesterday, and gave us a briefing, and said that tomorrow—that's today—y'all haul—well, I can't rightly say exactly what it was he said. Get over to Rancho Miraflores, is what he meant. Pretty fast too, he said.'

'Okay,' she snapped, 'so here you are. And now what? What did he tell you to do when you got here?'

'Everything that needs doing,' replied John.—or was it Jim? 'Left it up to us, he did. Course, we've had a lot of years experience.'

I'll just bet you have, Stacey thought, as she assessed them. Neither one looked to be older than twenty-one. Years of experience? Oh well. 'And who's going to pay for all this?'

'Well, ma'am, if you won't take it too poorly, it seems your husband, he arranged it all. Mind if we mosey along and get at it? We brought our own *remuda*.'

'Don't ask me anything,' Stacey told them. 'I don't have any answers. Lunch will be at twelve-thirty, and you'll eat in the house with us. The bunkhouse hasn't been used for eight or ten years, but you can't put your horses in the barn—that's been kept up.'

She could hardly help smiling at them. Their grins were infectious. But after they had gone she stomped into the house. I'm going to call that man, she told herself grimly, and chew him up one side and down the other. The nerve of him!

Her hand was halfway to the telephone when all the pieces began to fit together. She fell back into her chair and the giggles started to come. What's the matter with me, she lectured, is that I can't stand being done good to! Which, despite the poor English, seemed to sum it all up. She put the telephone down, and was still laughing when her aunt came through from the kitchen. 'Can we feed two more?' asked Stacey, still trying to control the giggles. 'It seems we've hired a drill-crew and a couple of ranch hands.'

'No problem at all,' Aunt Ellen responded. 'It just might liven things up around here.'

'I'll liven things up,' Stacey retorted, 'just as soon as I can get my hands on Harry Marsden. I'll liven things up, believe me! I wonder why he doesn't call! Darn that man!'

She did hear from him that day, but the message was not one she wanted to receive. It was four o'clock in the afternoon, and the sky was growing darker. Far to the north-west there were flashed of lightning splitting the clouds. The telephone rang—not the series of repetitive sounds that one expects, but rather one long ring, and then silence. Stacey pulled herself away from the window where she had been watching Mr Steuben at work. The old man had consulted charts, inspected gradients, surveyed particular points—and then whipped out a dowsing rod to determine just where to drill. Stacey was still chuckling as she moved towards the telephone. She picked it up and offered a tentative 'hello'.

'Mrs Marsden?' the coolly modulated voice asked. 'Mrs Stacey Marsden?'

'Yes,' she responded automatically, 'speaking.'

'I have a message for you from your husband.'

'I—' It took her just a moment to think herself into the right mental posture. I've got to be more careful, she moaned. I'm almost beginning to believe it myself! 'Yes, go ahead.'

'Mr Marsden is in Houston. He hopes to return immediately, but the weather is bad for flying, and it may take some time. He asked me to call and inform you that his grandmother passed away this afternoon.'

'Oh, how terrible!' Stacey returned. A picture of the tiny frail form in the bed, clinging to her hand, fingering her rings, flashed into her mind. And the smile that had fixed itself on the worn face as she closed her eyes.

'Did she ever come out of the coma?' she asked tearfully.

'No.' For a moment the voice had sounded as if it cared, but suddenly it became all business again. 'Mr Marsden asks that you come to Waco for the wake and the funeral. He also asked me to repeat a peculiar statement. He said I was to tell you that he badly needed support. Does that sound right?'

'Yes,' Stacey responded softly, 'I understand. Does he want me to come to Waco right away?'

'Oh no, Mrs Marsden. He intends to come for you, and just as soon as he can.'

'I understand. If you talk to him again, please tell him I'll be waiting for him.'

The thunderstorm broke over Gatesville about six o'clock that evening, and although she peered out the windows at least every fifteen minutes, until Aunt Ellen began to complain, Staccy knew that no aircraft would want to challenge that sky. In between trips to the window, she sorted through her meagre wardrobe, and packed what looked presentable into a single suitcase. She had nothing in black, and that bothered her. The image of that frail old woman, clinging desperately to life until her dreams were fulfilled, stuck in her mind. She knew that no matter what others thought, she would mourn.

There were no large stores in her immediate area. Pidcoke was the nearest, but hardly a major shopping centre. Gatesville, the county seat, was farther away, and on a stormy Friday night it too might have little to offer. Stacey did what she had learned to do over the past few weeks—she put the problem aside, and went for a hot bath.

Steaming hot, this bath, misting the bathroom,

fogging the mirrors, colouring her skin a brilliant pink as she slipped into it and relaxed. Bath bubbles played around her, releasing lavender fragrance into the air. She scooped up a handful of the suds, inhaled, then lay back in the tub. Wild dreams. Her hand played sensuously up and down her side, from curve of hip to peak of breast, while she dreamed—of him, of course. Of my husband, she thought, who has rights and privileges no other man has had—and who knows me better than anyone in the world. A man who—suddenly the trend of her thought bothered her, and she sat up primly, rebuking herself for such wild wanderings. Her *temporary* husband! But wouldn't it be nice if it were real, and he were here? Her hand wandered again, stirring emotions she had never expected. Her head dropped back onto the rest, and a smile played at her mouth.

All of which blocked her ears to the sound of heavy footsteps on the stairs. The unlocked bathroom door burst open without ceremony, and very suddenly he was there!

'Well—really!' she spluttered. There was not a towel within reach, and she had left all her clothing in the bedroom. Seething, she sank down under the cover of the soap bubbles. 'What in the world are you doing, breaking in here like that!' she shouted at him.

'Hey,' he said, with a tired sound in his voice, 'your aunt said you were in the tub and would probably camp out there for another hour unless somebody stirred you. So I'm stirring.'

'You could have knocked!' she snarled at him. 'I'm not selling tickets. This isn't an exhibition!'

'You don't know what you're saying,' he chuckled. 'It's some beautiful sight, Kitten. Come on—I had to drive all the way from Houston, and I'm tired. Millie called to tell me she was being mobbed by calls and problems. Boy, do I need a wife!' He pulled one of the huge bath towels from the rack and held it out, widespread. 'Come on now, Kitten, into the towel and let's get you dry so we can hit the road.'

There was mutiny in her eyes. 'Don't call me that,' she snarled. 'The least you could do is get my name right!'

Harry paid no attention to the outburst, but jiggled the towel at her a couple of times, as a matador might do in the arena. '*Ola, toro!*'

'I'll *toro* you!' she snarled. She scrambled at the sides of the slippery tub and barely managed to throw herself on the floor at his feet.

'Well, that wasn't much of a charge,' he said solemnly, staring down at her quivering anger without a twinge of concern.

'Why, you—arrogant—conceited—' She was so angry she stuttered. She tried to get up without using her hands, which were vainly busied trying to cover her breasts.

'I do believe you're right,' he drawled. 'My grandmother used to say exactly the same things. Pig-headed, too—one of her favourites. Pig-headed arrogant conceited male!'

'I'm sorry.' Stacey could see the torment behind his eyes, the strain-lines on his cheeks. 'I didn't think,' she said quietly, and got up gracefully. With equal grace he enfolded her in the towel, covering her completely from neck to toe. He pulled her back against him and leaned over her shoulder.

'This is no time for tears—that's what she told me, love. She had her time in this life—a long fruitful time—and she was ready to go on, convinced there's a better life beyond. So no tears. Now's the time for us to remember what she was, and pray success on her journey. All right?'

'All right,' she whispered. There was a great comfort to be gained, leaning back against him, letting his strong muscles take over all the labour of living. She recalled again that frail little body, the parchment face, those eyes boring into her, and the promise she had made just before his grandmother slipped into her final coma. 'I'm ready for whatever you want me to do,' she sighed.

Downstairs, her bag in his hand, she stopped him. 'I won't let you drive all that distance back without something to eat,' she insisted. Harry argued, but she stood firm. 'It's seven o'clock at night,' she nagged at him. 'Your grandmother is dead. Surely another hour won't make that much difference?'

He gave in, but not too graciously, sitting at the kitchen table making small talk to Aunt Ellen while Stacey wrestled with a steak, and warmed some chips she had taken from the freezer. With coffee bubbling on the stove, she set a man-sized plate in front of him, and sat back to watch while his temper improved in direct ratio to the disappearance of the food before him.

'Hits the spot,' he gasped at last. 'Second best meal in Texas, that. Second only to—'

'I know,' she laughed. 'My father was one of you too. Second only to barbecue. Drink your coffee.'

'I keep forgetting that you're a hometown girl,' he said. 'Some day you must let me throw you a barbecue. How are the Morgan boys doing?'

'I don't know, do I?' His change of subject was too much for her tired mind. 'You shift topics faster than a rattler sheds its skin. Darn you, how am I supposed to know how the Morgan boys are doing? The last time I checked they were fixing a leak in the bunkhouse roof. I don't know if they got it done, I don't know if they intend to stay here, I don't know what or when they get to eat—and most of all, Mr Marsden. I don't know what the devil they're doing here!'

'That certainly ought to keep you busy for a while.' He smiled wearily, then seemed to shrug his shoulders and get back into high gear. 'Come on now, let's get hustling. Aunt Ellen, you can expect her when you see her. And don't you go worrying about the Morgan boys. They've had their instructions. No worries, right?'

Although Aunt Ellen had made her peace with

Stacey, she still did not understand the man who had brought about all the change. She stared at his face, as if trying to read some concealed message there. 'I don't understand, but I'll try not to worry,' she said.

The sky was spitting rain by the time they settled into the big Mercedes. Harry tossed her bag on to the back seat and settled in behind the wheel. 'One bag, Stacey? You're travelling light?'

'I don't mean to,' she said, watching his skilled hands take them out on to Route 116, heading north towards the junction with Highway 84. 'It's just that—well, I never did have many clothes, and I don't have a driver's licence, so I just can't run into town when I want to. And, Harry,' she touched his knee to be sure of his attention, 'I don't have anything black. I suppose it's proper to be dressed in black?'

'I hadn't thought about that.' He took his attention away from the road long enough to smile at her. 'Having a wife is very complicated, isn't it?' She returned the smile weakly, wanting to yell at him, *Not half as complicated as having a husband!* But she stifled the words. He lifted one wrist to consult his watch. 'Eight-fifteen now. Everything in Waco will be closed at nine, unless—I know. Hand me the telephone, girl.'

The instrument was hidden inside a compartment between their seats. Look at this, Stacey told herself. I own oil wells and don't have a dress to wear. He works for a living managing something, and rides around with a telephone in his car! She handed him the instrument, then moved as far away from him as she could.

The downpour was almost obliterating the road markers when they finally reached the main highway. They ghosted through Gatesville as if it were a deserted city. The only lights to be seen were in two drugstores. There was some sign of life at the County Courthouse as they went through the tree-lined square in the centre of the city, and then out the other side, with a straight run to Waco. Harry drove one-handed, carrying on some

argument on the telephone. When he put it down there
was a smile of satisfaction on his face.

'It's hard to get what you want on a rainy Friday
night,' he told her.

'I don't really believe that,' she returned. 'You always
get what you want—at least that's the way it seems to
me. What now?'

He ran one tired hand through his hair, and shrugged
his shoulders to relax the driving tensions. 'It's like most
everything,' he chuckled. 'It's not what you know, but
who you know. The answer to our problem is Dillards.
It's a Department Store at the Richland Mall, right
ahead of us, at the intersection of Waco Drive and
Franklin Street. The manager and I went to school
together. Good old boys—that sort of thing. And he's
willing to stay open until we get there. If they don't have
a black dress for you I'll eat my hat.'

As it turned out, at seventy miles an hour they arrived
in the mall shortly before closing time, and found assist-
ance, and a suitable black dress without a bit of trouble.
'It's severely simple,' the saleswoman told Stacey.
'Something for—not necessarily for funerals, you know.
It should do.'

It did look simple of line, knee-length, with a high
demure collar. It was not until she tried it on that she
discovered how closely it clung, how tantalising it
looked. But Harry, his mind on other things, gave it a
quick okay, then insisted on a matching hat and veil.

'But I'm not close family,' she protested. 'That would
be overdoing it.'

'How much closer can you get?' he whispered.
'You're my wife. I'm her only grandson; all the rest are
distant aunts and uncles. Besides, Grandmother was a
locally famous woman. The press will be there, and who
knows how many friends, and friends of friends. You'll
be one of the stars, girl, and don't you forget it.'

'How could I?' she groaned. It was almost impossible
to win an argument with him while at the same time

keeping up with what the saleswoman was saying. 'I'm beginning to wish I'd taken up Drama when I went to Saint Anselm's. But you're not fooling me, Harry *dear*. What you want to do is keep me out of sight without actually hiding me. Isn't that it?'

'Women!' He threw up his hands, and gained the immediate support of the store manager. 'And besides the hat and veil, while we're at it, how about a few more odds and ends? My wife has come home almost thread-bare. If you don't mind?'

'As long as we're here, we might as well go whole hog,' the manager returned. 'Providing out Mrs Lord here can spare the time?' With visions of commissions running through her head, 'our Mrs Lord' was more than willing to spare the whole night. And so when they headed towards the door, and out into the darkened Mall, it took all four of them to carry the packages.

The car started with a grumble. 'Wet wiring,' Harry told Stacey. 'It was a real gully-washer out towards Houston, and hasn't gotten better since. Now, one more stop, and we're off for the house.'

'I don't mind,' she affirmed. 'It's you I'm worried about. Do you want me to drive?'

'I thought you said you didn't have a licence?'

'I don't, but that doesn't mean I can't drive, for goodness' sakes. I've driven all kinds of things around the ranch. I started when I was twelve.'

'I just bet you did!' There was a tinge of sarcasm in his answer. She sat back in her seat and folded both hands in her lap. And that's the last time you'll get an offer from me, she muttered under her breath.

'What was that?'

'Keep your eyes on the road. All we need to make my life complete is a road accident.'

'Women!' Harry groaned.

'Hah! Men!' She squirmed just a little bit further away to demonstrate her absolute and complete indepen-dence, then spoiled it all by giggling at him. He drove

with exaggerated care down Franklin, took a slow right
turn on 18th Street, crossed the railroad tracks, then
made a sharp left on Clay, passing the Municipal
Stadium and going on down past 7th Street, where he
pulled up in the middle of the block.

'This is it,' he explained as he shut off the engine. 'Was
madame satisfied with my driving?'

'Yes. This is what?'

'Our home,' he chuckled, and Stacey looked out of
the window. Another gust of rain struck, and his hand
restrained her. 'No sense running between the rain-
drops. We'd both drown.'

It made some sense—the bit about the rain, that was.
But a home? She peered out the window at the building.
It was neither new nor old, one of the units built in the
era when everything had to be glass. Not too big, either,
for that matter; eight or nine floors, as best she could
guess. Neat, but not ostentatious. Perhaps it might give
her some clue as to what Harry did for a living. So why
not ask?

'What do you do for a living, Harry?'

'Oh, this and that,' he answered lightly. 'I manage
things. I have a little organisation up on the top floor.
We do—well, I guess you might call it odd jobs.'

'Oh. You don't use the whole building?'

'No, Stacey, there are other tenants. The rain's letting
up. Come on, let's give it a whirl.'

He was out of the car and around to her door before
she could shape another question. His hand palmed her
elbow and hurried her through the drizzle, and in at
double doors which gave access to a small lobby. A
security guard greeted them at the desk, making small
talk about rain and rheumatism as Harry signed the
book. While the two of them were busy, Stacey looked
around and found a building directory. Floors numbered
one through five belonged to Parsons Oil Explorations.
Floors six and seven were the property of Westland
Cattle Associates. Floor eight belonged to the Federal

Electronics Corporation. Floor nine was the property of—ah—Marsden Management Corporation. And then there was a penthouse, with no names attached.

'What's the matter, somebody walking over your grave?' Harry's hand was on her elbow again, as he hurried her over to the elevator bank, pushed a button, and got instant response—of course, she told herself. Even the elevators wouldn't dare make *him* wait!

Don't say a word, she lectured herself. Isn't life crazy enough already with what you know? Why make it worse by learning something more? So he makes a living. It's a nice building, but set squarely between the railroad tracks and an elevated super-highway. Not exactly the classiest neighbourhood in the world. And— of course! Parsons Oil. He shares a building with them. No wonder he could get all kinds of information! 'I'll bet you a nickel to a doughnut he knows a dozen secretaries in the right places!' she remarked.

She hadn't meant for that to come out—not in the confines of a slow elevator. Harry looked at her quizzically, but before he had time to pursue the subject the elevator stopped and the doors opened. At floor number ten, the blinking light said.

'Did we miss a floor someplace?' Stacey asked cautiously.

'Not that I know of. Downstairs is where I work. This is where I—I mean this is where we live. Come on, I'll only be a minute or two!'

She dragged her feet, wondering just how far into whatever mess there was she had finally stepped. 'You— you live here? I thought you lived—Rosedale—your grandmother's house? The servants, the horses, and—'

The door was controlled by some sort of electronic lock. He merely placed his palm on a plate by its side, above the bell, and everything slid open for them. 'You're just a little incoherent tonight,' he chuckled. 'Maybe a drink will settle you down.'

'I—' He was pushing her ahead of him through a tiny corridor and into a spacious living room that faced out over the lights of the city. Rain drummed at the wide glass panes. A sunken centre held couches and stuffed chairs. Around the elevated rim were tables, a few occasional chairs, books, and a huge desk. In the near wall, a fireplace sparkled with a gas fire. A pair of wide stairs led up to a half-landing, where other closed doors shut off the view. 'If—if you're having one?' she sighed.

'Sure. Scotch on the rocks for me, but something non-alcoholic for you. Alcohol and Valium don't mix, and you'll be another six months getting it all out of your system.'

'Which doesn't leave me much choice, does it? How about a Coke?'

Harry fumbled through a stack of papers while she answered. When he looked up his grin was back, that wide infectious grin which had so held her when first they met. 'Coke?' he laughed. 'Well, I don't think I have any of that. How about a Doctor Pepper?'

'Oh, you!' There was a pillow close at hand. She threw it at him, then dodged around to the other side of the room. 'You didn't bring me here to look at papers and offer me drinks,' she said. 'So just why did we come?'

'Smart,' he said solemnly. 'Can't pull the wool over your eyes, huh?'

'Watch that talk,' she giggled. 'This is cattle country.'

'You've seen too many John Wayne movies,' he returned. 'I do have a good reason for bringing you here, Stacey.' He came around the room and touched her hand lightly. 'This is where I live. This is where you've been living. When we get out to Grandmother's place, as far as all the people out there know, you've just come from this penthouse with me. So I wanted you to have a look around, to get the feel of this place, before we go on. Satisfied?'

'Harry, you are some great conspirator, aren't you? You think of everything. It would never have crossed my mind!'

'Of course not. That's what I'm here for—to do all the devious thinking. Ready for the Grand Tour?' And off she went again, tugging after him as he moved at full speed towards the stairs. She stumbled as her foot missed the first step, but his hand sustained and tugged and urged. Onward and upward, she laughed to herself. Will I ever get to move at a normal speed again?

The first door at the half-landing opened into a massive bathroom, all blue and white tile, with a sunken tub in one corner, and a barrel-shaped hot tub in the other. Stacey took one look and almost swallowed her tongue. For more than two weeks Harry had put up with the old dingy bathroom at the ranch, with a tub whose enamel was cracking, and whose four supporting claw legs were weak enough to rock!

'Care to try it out?' It was a sarcastic offering, she thought, but then again, could she ever be sure of a man like Harry? Just in case, she returned a polite refusal and he led her back to the landing.

The second door opened to another flight of stairs that opened into a single circular bedroom that took her breath away. The room had no walls. Windows completed a great circle around her, allowing three hundred and sixty-degree look at the city. A few scatter pillows occupied strategic sections of the thick-pile carpet. In the middle of the room a huge circular bed was set up on a pedestal. Storage space was provided by low cabinets, built under the windows, and below the level of the bed. There was no other furniture.

'Watch this,' he said gleefully—like a kid with a brand new toy, Stacey told herself. Look at how much he enjoys showing me—this what? His finger moved a dial on the wall, and the windows gradually turned opaque, shutting out the driving rain. 'There's a control like this on the bed, too. Hop on to the bed, Stacey. Nobody will believe you if you haven't tried the bed.'

She looked over at him, confused. Try the bed? Now what? she thought. Is this the old story—lie down on my bed, lady, and we'll have a long talk? Warily she walked around the side of the bed farthest from him and sank gingerly down into the absorbing softness of the thing. It rolled slightly beneath her, readjusting to her form as she moved.

'A water bed?' she gasped.

'Best in the West,' he chuckled. 'It gives a fine night's rest.'

I'll just bet it does, she thought. If it wiggles when you sit down on it, what the devil happens if—if something more athletic takes place? A girl could get seasick in a place like this. Look at him—he's waiting for me to ask, and I'll be darned if I will!

'Lie back,' he instructed. 'You haven't seen anything yet!'

'I—I don't suppose I have,' she offered weakly. Almost automatically her feet came up off the floor and coiled themselves up. She leaned back towards the pillows, just as he joined her from the other side. Keep a respectable distance, her nerves screamed. She crowded over towards the edge. There was no need. The bed was big enough for six. A family could fit in with ease!

She slowly lowered her head back until the pillows supported her. It *was* comfortable. But why was Harry grinning like some jackass, waiting carefully for her to settle down? I won't ask him. Let him be a smart aleck!

He was prone, but his head was held up on one bent elbow. With exaggerated movements, his hand moved to a metal plate under his pillow, and pushed a button. Nothing seemed to happen, until his fingers moved to a dial beside the panel of buttons, and the windows slowly became transparent again. And there was definitely something wrong! The lights of the city were very slowly circling around them—or—no, the bed itself was slowly rotating, so that someone in the bed, on a clear day, could see a panorama of the entire city.

'It's hard to see because of the storm,' he said. 'But here beginneth the reading from the First Book of Waco, Texas.' Before her eyes the city marched very slowly in review. 'You're looking south now,' he commented, in his best tourist-guide voice. 'Those lights are cars on the Kultgen Freeway, Interstate 35, and now—we're moving eastward, those lights are at the campus of Baylor University. My company lives on brain power, and we draw most of that right off the campus graduate school. Now, that's the light reflecting off Lake Brazos, and next to it you can see a tiny part of Fort Fisher, the original Texas Ranger camp in this part of the state. Most of that is a museum now. And there—as we move north, that's the Convention Center, the Municipal Building, the Mall, and then, all the way around our circle, that's the Waco Municipal Stadium. And way beyond that is Baylor Stadium. You'll have to come up some sunny afternoon to see it all. It takes a full fifteen minutes for the bed to make one revolution.'

A fierce burst of envy—no, jealousy—struck at her. Obviously he didn't spend his afternoons up here riding his bed around in circles, alone. How many other women had seen this sight—or perhaps had been too busy to see the sights? I'll bet it takes considerably less than fifteen minutes for *him* to complete one revolution. All those poor, poor women. I wish I was one of them!

'Daydreaming?' he intruded.

'I don't know,' she stammered, embarrassed by her own thoughts. 'It's just—I don't understand who would be questioning me about your—your bed—and your apartment, and things. Am I going to be on the griddle some place?'

'I don't know one way or the other,' he sighed. 'All this doesn't strike you as the least bit romantic?'

'Not in the least,' she lied. 'It looks like a move-lot seduction scene. If my lesson is complete, could we perhaps get going?'

'Damn!' Once again she had found the wrong phrase, the wrong answer. But if he had been asking serious questions, she just did not understand them. Very suddenly it became chilly, as if the air-conditioners had been turned up full blast. Harry got up out of the bed, leaving her to rock in the wavelets by herself. He stalked around the bed to where she was barely clinging to the edge.

'If that's not romantic,' he said determinedly, 'how about this!' He dropped down almost on top of her, and as she opened her mouth to protest, his lips sealed her off. Closed down her entire world, and let in a concentrated circle of spark and flame that chased echoes up and down her spine, and back to her hip, where one of his hands rested. She made a futile effort to struggle against him. He put down the rebellion without a bit of trouble, and returned to the attack.

Stacey closed her eyes, her frame shaking in anticipation. And again the sparks, the flame, the riot of sensation as his warm lips challenged hers, invading her mouth without mercy, without challenge. She stiffened for a moment, then gave it up, relaxing in the fury of the storm he was creating with his lips. When he finally pulled away from her she was unable to move. He watched, like a heron watches the shallows, waiting. When her breathing apparatus finally settled down she ran a nervous hand through her hair, brushing it back from her perspiring forehead.

'How about that?' Harry asked of the room in general.

She stared up at him, having trouble focusing her eyes. How about that? Is that all he can say about the quake that shattered my whole world? How about that? The bitterness crept in under the sweet. Colour me green, for jealousy, she screamed at herself. How many others have there been? One thing's for sure, the scenery is a waste. None of them could ever looked out the window while *he* was working at his scductive best!

CHAPTER FIVE

It was after midnight when they drove up to the old house on the hill. The storm had abated, thundering off towards the Gulf coast, leaving behind it the heady smell of fresh-cleaned air, and the tang of wild sage, damp earth, the fragrance of oleanders, and the dusty dry smell of cedar. One star, no more, peeped through the tail of clouds. One light, a small yellow bug-light, gleamed at the front door.

'They've all gone to bed,' commented Harry, sounding as if he were astonished by the whole idea. 'We'll have to struggle with this lot by ourselves.' He was standing outside the rear door of the car, peering in at the pile of boxes that littered the back seat.

'Well, it was all your idea,' Stacey teased. 'All I ever wanted was the black dress.'

'All right, hush now.' He gave an exaggerated sigh, and she searched his face. The closer they came to the house, the more solemn he had become, almost as if the mansion was stretching out dark fingers to embrace him. 'Do your darn best best to refrain from being a smart aleck, will you? You go first and open the doors, and I'll struggle with your paraphernalia. And don't make a sound. There's nothing I hate to face worse than an aroused household. Millie is really a witch without her sleep.'

'Me too,' she told him, then ducked away as he swung one heavy hand in the direction of her bottom. 'OK, I'm going. Are you sure you don't want me to take some of those little boxes?'

'Yes, I'm sure,' he snapped back. 'Why did I ever get married?' That last statement was addressed to the one bright star.

'How should I know?' she said wistfully. 'Probably because I'm so beautiful?' This time she was unable to avoid his hand, and retreated towards the door, rubbing her injured flank.

It took three trips up the stairs, some light squabbling, and one or two minor catastrophes involving furniture being in the wrong places. So that made it two in the morning before she managed to shoo him out of the door, strip off her clothes, and fall wearily into bed. The day had seemed ten years long.

A dream possessed her. Somehow or another she was staked out on a rotating platform, and an unrecognisable monster was about to turn her into a virgin sacrifice, using the knife method. She tossed and turned, woke and went back to sleep, twisted the sheets into knots, and was unable to fall asleep again until just before dawn. And in his next reappearance the monster was using his knife to tickle her nose. Stacey pushed one eye open warily, and the monster became Harry, using a tiny feather rather than a knife.

'It's eight o'clock,' he said very solemnly. 'Time to get up. There are lots of things to take care of today.'

'Nobody gets up at eight o'clock, Harry. And if you think I'm one of those country girls who get up with the chickens—well, think again. My father hated chickens. And I'm a night person.' He tickled her nose again.

'Damn you,' she said in her grumpiest voice, and rolled over on her side, with her back to him. He came around to the other side of the bed and knelt down on the carpet. His face was barely inches from hers. She managed to get both eyes open. There was no smile on his face. In fact, all the craggy lines were back—worry lines, as she knew by now.

She stretched out one hand from under the sheet and pushed back the lock of unruly hair that kept falling over his forehead. Deep in his eyes she could see the pain, rigidly suppressed. Oh God, she thought, another proud

Texan. It just isn't the thing for a Texan to cry, no matter how much pain it alleviates.

Ignoring her skimpy nightgown, she sat up and cradled his head between her hands. 'Your grandmother?' she asked hesitantly. The corner of his mouth twitched upward very briefly.

'That's one of the reasons why I've never married, Stacey,' he said. 'You're too discerning by far. Yes, my grandmother.'

'Tell me about it,' she offered, hoping to help him find release.

'There's nothing to tell,' he said gruffly. He stood up and turned away from her. She slipped out of bed to stand beside him. 'My mother and father died when I was young,' he continued. 'Grandma stepped in and raised me.'

'And also her godchild?'

'Yes, and also Lisette. End of story. She was a grand old lady. I've long since adjusted to the idea that I was going to lose her, but it didn't really strike me until last night—until we came on to the property. I had this crazy feeling that she was up there someplace on the turret, watching to see what I would do about things. Oh Lord, this is all nonsense. There are a million things to do, and you're the mistress of the house. Let's go downstairs to the kitchen and have some breakfast first.'

End of a confidence! Stacey felt suddenly bereft. For a moment Harry had offered her a part of himself, and then as quickly snatched it away. She watched as he stalked off towards the bathroom. He was wearing only a pair of pyjama bottoms, and his bronze back made him look like a Greek god. Everything brown, except for that line of white at his midriff, above the pyjamas, that marked his slender waist and emphasised his narrow buttocks. He moved like an athlete, graceful, flowing. But not once did he look back as the bathroom door closed behind him.

Stacey sat up in the bed, no longer mindful of her own

concerns. He had called on her for support, and she must give it. The clothes she had shed the night before were scattered around the room. She picked them up, slipped into her robe, made a simple selection of undies, jeans, and blouse, and went out into the hall to find another bathroom.

They were both downstairs within fifteen minutes, just in time to catch Millie as she placed two loaded plates on a tray. 'Oh my, you startled me!' the elderly housekeeper gasped. 'I was going to bring breakfast up. You two have hardly had a honeymoon at all. You need a little pampering.'

'But I've already had that,' Stacey laughed. 'Have you ever seen Harry's apartment?'

'Ah, that!' laughed Millie as she removed the tray and set two places at the kitchen table. 'You want to watch that stuff, girl. Sodom and Gomorrah, that's what that's all about. How in the world do you ever get any sleep with that bed going around in circles?'

'We manage,' Harry broke in. 'Pull up a mug of coffee and sit a spell, Millie. There's a lot of thinking to be done.'

He held Stacey's chair for her. She slipped into it and flashed him a thank-you smile. Millie, suddenly very serious, went over to the big gas cooker in the corner and refilled her mug. 'You've made all the arrangements downtown?' she asked as she came back and sat down at the table. 'Eat before it gets cold.'

Almost automatically Stacey's fork came into play. 'There's not much outside arranging to be done,' said Harry between mouthfuls of scrambled eggs. 'It's been expected for so long that we've had all the plans made. No, the big problem will be right here in the house. I expect some of the family members will start to trickle in today. I had my secretary make all the calls last night. And, of course, they'll all demand to be accommodated here at the mansion. And that puts the monkey on your back, Stacey. Yours and Millie's, of course.'

'She can do it.' The older woman patted Stacey's hand. 'Young, but she's got guts, Harry. I still don't know how you lucked out with this one, after those crackpots you usually bring around. The only thing—' She looked Stacey up and down in a critical fashion. 'The only thing is that all that family of yours will expect *her* to do things for them. You know, meet them at the door, see to their rooms, preside over meals—all that. And for that, little Mrs, you've got to start wearing dresses.'

'I—I have some,' Stacey stammered. 'And I'll—try. If y'all will help?'

'We'll help,' promised Millie. 'Fill us in on the general plan, Harry.'

'OK. Tomorrow we'll have the family wake. The day after there's a public one scheduled. I understand that the Governor intends to come.' He looked over at Stacey's surprised face, and took both her hands in his.

'Grandmother was a famous lady in her time,' he told her. 'There'll be a lot of her friends come—those that she hasn't outlived. The Governor's father was one of her favourite beaux before she settled on grandfather. Where was I?'

'The public wake the day after tomorrow,' Millie threw in.

'Oh, yes. The funeral will be on Friday. She wanted to be buried from her old parish church in town, the one she and Grandfather attended before he made a mint of money and moved out here—the First Lutheran, that is. And the burial will be beside her husband. She wanted it simple.'

'So then there won't be any trouble,' Stacey asked.

'Oh, there'll be trouble,' he sighed. 'After the funeral. Grandma was a very rich woman, and there'll be aunts and uncles all over the place, looking for what they can get. They couldn't see their way clear to come and visit when she was alive, but now they'll be in on top of us like a bunch of sharks. Oh yes, there'll be more than enough trouble for all, believe you me. I don't know what it contains, but her will is only one page long. There'll be a gnashing of teeth when it's read. Stick with me, wife!'

The few days went by quickly. Stacey found herself lost in the mass of family that poured in, all demanding rooms in the mansion. She played her part as mistress in style. In the face of the invasion Harry hired two women from Valley View to come in by the day. Stacey pitched in to help in the kitchen, too, in addition to supervising the new help.

Harry commanded her to the public wake. She shrugged herself into the black dress, crammed her hair up under an unaccustomed hat, and sat patiently at his side while mourners in their dozens passed by the bier. By the time the Governor arrived she was too tired to notice what was going on. All the newspapers were on hand, referring to it as 'the passing of an era.'

The next day, under a bright Texas sun, they buried the old lady in the family plot in the old part of the cemetery, beside the lost lover of her youth, who had preceded her in death by more than twenty years. And then it was over.

So much panoply and ceremony, Stacey sighed to herself as they were driven back to the house. So much, for a tiny woman whom she had seen for scarcely an hour, before she slipped away into a coma. If it had not been love that Harry's grandmother had engendered in her, at least it was respect. She leaned back against the seat, folded her black veil up out of the way, and dabbed at her eyes. His hand came over and covered hers, resting in her lap. A firm squeeze, a signal of shared grief and comfort. She accepted it for what it was, and closed her eyes.

As it turned out, those days of the wake and funeral were the peaceful days, for no sooner were they all back at the mansion than pandemonium set in. Uncle Clarence—the one with the broken nose and the loud voice—was insisting that the two paintings in the study belonged to him, while three other couples disputed his right. Harry disabused them all, warning that the estate would be distributed according to the will, and in no other way.

'They're both Renoirs,' he told her grimly as they made their way up to their rooms to change. 'Everybody wants what Grandmother had, but none of them were ever willing to work for it. You're lucky, Stacey, to be from such a small family.'

'Am I?' She turned away from him, not willing for him to see the additional tear in her eye. Apart from Aunt Ellen, she told herself fiercely, I've got nobody—and he's complaining because he's got a million aunts and uncles! So maybe they *do* squabble a little. Shaking her head, she snatched up some work clothes and ran into the bedroom to change. She walked by him without looking, and dashed for the kitchen.

'No need for that,' Millie reprimanded minutes later. 'We got caterers to come in. There's all sorts of food set up in the dining room.'

'And all sorts of relatives,' muttered Stacey. 'Before the funeral they all looked so—nice. And now, Lord love us, I'm afraid to go by one of them for fear they'll bite me.'

'If they do you'll get rabies,' Millie commented. 'What do you really want in here?'

'I need some work, Millie. Some hard physical work, to make me forget.'

'Me too,' her older companion said softly. 'Twenty years I've been in this house. I wasn't much older than you are now when I come. Twenty years; it's hard to forget. Why don't we clean the silver before one of those—relatives—steals it all.'

And that was the start of another week. A week that progressed from silver polishing to general house-cleaning, despite the crowded conditions. 'Anything to keep your hands busy,' Millie said. 'A couple of solid weeks at hard labour, and then things will be back to—well, whatever normal is going to be around here in the future.'

Whatever normal is going to be? Stacey thought about that often during the nights that followed. She and Harry had settled into a routine: a display of moderate affection during the day—a few hugs, a kiss or two, a walk hand in hand. Nothing more. And then early retirement behind the closed door of their bedroom suite.

'Where, I suppose, they all think we're living it up,' grumbled Harry, as he tried to make himself comfortable in one of the spindly chairs. Stacey could hardly suppress a giggle. He was a big man, and looked so out of place in this feminine room. And yet, to foster the image, all his clothes shared the closet with hers. His shaving gear cluttered up the bathroom, and occasionally the smell of one of his cigars would fog the whole room. And there he sat, trying to distribute his weight on the little chair, while he read the day's paper.

Strange, that was, for a man who did—what the devil *does* he do for a living? she asked herself for the hundredth time; somehow she felt it would break her luck to ask *him*. Not raise horses! He had finally admitted that the pure-bred Arabs out in the paddock were his. But not a profitable business. He kept trying to explain to her what a tax loss was, to no avail. Somehow it all was too much of a puzzle. 'A penny saved is a penny earned'— That made sense. But not this other idea.

So Harry gave up explaining, and sat there, running through the pages of the Waco paper, the Dallas paper, and the *Wall Street Journal*. He was a sound-reader; whenever he came across an interesting paragraph he would hum contentedly. A story that displeased would bring a sharp 'Hmmmp!' And occasionally a story would be so hard to take that he would rip that page out of the paper and throw it into the waste basket.

My husband, Stacey lectured herself, and the idea brought a wistful sigh. It's only make-believe, of course. And I'm getting good at it, aren't I? Maybe I should start a company? 'Bronfield Rent-a-Bride?' That didn't sound too bad.

'You've lost a button on your shirt,' she commented.

'Ah.' Well, that was better than being totally ignored. She took out her sewing kit and began to match buttons. His paper rattled, and she looked up to find him staring at her over its top. A piercing stare, that seemed all-encompassing, as she fumbled with the needle, licked the end of the thread, and tried for the third time to force it through the needle's eye. I'm out of practice, the practical side of her mind told her. Like hell you are, the other side prodded. Why are your hands shaking so much? Either fish or cut bait, girl. Throw his shirt on the floor and stamp on it, then run across the room and jump on him. That's what you really want!

She fought back the urge, biting at her lower lip. The thread finally condescended to go through the hole, and she picked up the button and started at it, keeping her head lowered so that her hair swung between them. The needle flashed prettily. Almost as if you knew what you were doing, she shouted at herself. Harry's paper dropped into his lap.

'We'll hear the will read tomorrow,' he said. 'Look at us—we're getting to be a regular pair, aren't we? Darby and Joan?' He tossed the papers aside, came over, and dropped a kiss on the top of her head. 'Me for bed,' he said, and went through the door into the adjoining room, the one in which he actually slept. Stacey watched his back as he disappeared. Darby and Joan? Who in the world were they? A tiny tear formed at the corner of her eye, ran down her cheek, and fell off on to the shirt clutched in her hand.

She looked down at the shirt, as if it were something she had never seen before. 'That's silly,' she mumbled to herself. 'Why would anyone sew a button on at the elbow?' It took her almost an hour to cut the threads and place the button where it belonged.

So they heard the will read in the morning—the

relatives, that was. Stacey managed to fight her way out of bed by seven, and was in the kitchen preparing breakfast by seven-thirty. Practically all the relatives were up, she noticed, as she carried a platter of ham and eggs into the dining room. They all turned to stare at her, as if she were some sort of superior servant. She flashed them a quick smile, and retreated to the kitchen.

'Like a bunch of vultures,' she muttered to Millie, who was starting another batch of scrambled eggs. 'They look at me as if they think I might inherit something of theirs!'

At nine o'clock Mr Simmons arrived. He looked to be too young to represent the august firm of Herrick, Portnoy, and Simmons. But he had the right papers in hand, and all the family followed him into the big double-parlour. The doors closed behind them.

Less than half an hour later both Stacey and Millie, sharing coffee in a pair of old mugs in the kitchen, heard the uproar. 'Forty people, all yelling at once,' commented Millie. 'It sounds as if the old lady did them *all* in!'

The doors of the parlour slammed open, and disgruntled people stamped their way into the hall. 'I'll contest the will,' Aunt Marion shrieked. 'She can't do this to us—we're family!' Nobody else offered to second the motion. They all seemed lost in their own private agonies. By lunch time every one of them had left, in a mad cacophony of protests and tyre-squealings. Young Mr Simmons stood on the porch with Harry to watch them go, then he flashed a tiny smile, and followed.

Stacey came out of hiding in a dark corner of the hall as soon as the lawyer's car started moving, and joined Harry on the porch. He looked down at her sombrely, then grinned, dropping a friendly arm over her shoulder.

'Thank God for you, my dear,' he sighed, and she shifted contentedly under the weight of his arm. 'And that's what *family* means.'

'You sound so cynical. Was it always this bad?' She

wanted to comfort him, but her lack of experience betrayed her effort.

'Bad? I don't really know.' His left hand squeezed her shoulder. 'But I wish that Grandmother had left the entire estate to charity, or something.' There was a touch of bitterness behind his words. She could read the anguish in his eyes. 'Do you know what she's done to us?'

Done to *us*? A little shivering thrill ran up Stacey's spine. *Us?* Have we come this far, Harry, you and I? 'No, I didn't hear,' she said softly. 'What?'

'She left the entire estate to be divided equally between myself and her godchild Lisette. I don't even know what her married name is now. Grandmother made her will almost a year ago, when I think she was despairing that I would ever get married. So there we have it. The entire estate to be shared between us, with two provisos. First, I'm charged with finding Lisette. Second, she and I must both live together for three months in the mansion before we can dispose of it. And I haven't the slightest idea where she is. I haven't known for almost five years!'

'I—' Stacey could not find the words. Harry would live in this sprawling house for three months with another woman. The child he had grown up with. The woman he had once loved? Out of the grave his grandmother had laid a commitment on him that could surely only lead to—stop! Stacey screamed at herself. I don't want to think about it! She turned away from him, cramming her fist in her mouth to stifle the sobs.

'Kitten?' His hand touched her shoulder again.

'Don't call me that!' she sobbed, and ran for her room. She stood against the closed door, shaking, her frame rocking back and forth on unsteady feet. The tears came silently, flowing like Niagara, but unable to wash away her woes. When she heard the footsteps in the hall she looked wildly around for a place to hide. The only locks available were on the bathroom door, and at that were only a pair of courtesy bolts. Nevertheless, they were something. Stacey shook her trembling feet loose from the rug to which they seemed glued, and ran for the bathroom. She could hear the bedroom door open behind her as she slammed the bolts home. Harry knocked twice.

'Stacey? Are you all right?'

'Yes,' she managed to force out of a hoarse throat. 'Please—'

'All right. Lunch will be in an hour. We have a lot to talk about.'

She leaned wearily against the wall, one hand clutching the towel rack for support. Yes, we have a lot to talk about, she thought, but only one of us is ready to listen. He thinks he's too old for me. As soon as he finds Lisette—Kitten—he'll fall back into the old pattern. And then they'll live here together, and propinquity will take care of the rest. Lord, I had a chance up to that point. But he has a charge from his grandmother to find that woman, and he will. It's no use. Maybe in fifty years, when I've finally grown up—but I can't wait. I've got to go now, while I've still got the courage!

Given a goal to work to, her mind responded. She put her ear to the door and heard nothing. Cautiously she unfastened the bolts and peered out. The bedroom was empty. Stacey hurried to the closet, pulled out her old suitcase, and opened it on the bed. Only your own clothing, her mind commanded. Her fingers skipped past all the delicate light finery Harry had bought her on that stormy night, and plucked out only her old dresses, dungarees, and slips. She crammed them into the case without thought to proper order, then emptied the drawers of her own plain cotton briefs, ignoring the piles of flimsy lace and silk that he had helped choose. Her heart seemed to block her throat as she shut the closet door against temptation, and locked her case.

She could hear them talking—Millie and Harry and Frank—as she stole down the staircase by the kitchen, and out of the front door. There were three cars parked beside the house. The Mercedes was too much for her, and the little red Sprite standing next to it was just as bad, but the battered old four-wheel-drive jeep was just her style, and the key was in the ignition. It took several minutes for her to adjust the seat. The engine fired at the turn of the key. The gears screeched as she shifted, and she whirled the vehicle around, heading out to the highway.

The commotion from the house came to her ears. The back door slammed shut as someone came charging out. But her eyes were glued to the road. Despite all her boasting, her experience of driving on the farm had in no way prepared her for reality. She clenched her teeth, wrestled the heavy vehicle to the far right side of the road, and careered down it at full speed. As she approached the old cemetery at Keys she slowed down, looking for a way to the main highway. A quick jog at the Bosqueville corners eventually led her to Lake Shore Drive. She slowed down to twenty-five miles an hour, ignoring the host of beeping cars piling up behind her, and did her best to keep the heavy vehicle on the road. Eventually she picked up the Route 35 markers, and followed them up on to the divided highway.

She gave a great sigh of relief when she saw the unencumbered road stretching out in front of her, like a south-pointing arrow. The cars which had been tailing her all the way roared by, honking derisively as they went. Stacey wobbled her vehicle to the side of the road and stopped almost underneath the sign which said *No Stopping On Highway*. She was still fumbling for a tissue when the Texas Ranger car pulled up behind her, and an officer ambled over to where she sat, frozen at the wheel.

'I wasn't speeding,' she defended herself the moment he came up to the door. 'I wasn't!'

'No, ma'am.' He grinned a mouthful of white young teeth at her as he took off his dark glasses and whipped out a notebook. 'May I see your licence, please?'

Her face turned a brilliant red. 'I I don't seem to have it with me,' she mumbled, fumbling in her handbag as if there was something to find.

'But you're supposed to,' he responded gently. 'Didn't they tell you that when you got your licence?'

'No,' she whispered, 'they didn't tell me that.'

'That's strange,' he returned jovially. 'They're supposed to tell you. Well, where did you get your licence?'

'I—I don't have a licence,' she confessed, ducking her head.

His smile shrank just a bit. 'No licence,' he muttered to himself as he scribbled something in his book. 'But you do have the car's registration, I imagine. May I see that, please?'

'I—I don't have the car registration,' she answered in a very small, very timid voice.

'Don't tell me you stole the car?' He was joking, she knew, trying to reduce the tension he could read on her face.

'Yes.'

'Oh, brother!' The smile had gone completely. 'Please show me some identification.'

Stacey reached for her bag again, only to find that he had backed away from the car and drawn his revolver. 'I—I was just—I have a credit card,' she offered. He extended one hand carefully and took it.

'Stacey Bronfield,' he said. 'That's you?'

'I—yes, that's me. I—'

'And you live where?'

'In Coryelle County,' she responded, more terrified of that huge gun than she would care to admit. 'On the highway between Pidcoke and Gatesville.'

'And who did you steal the car from?'

'From—' It almost came out. From my husband. Oh Lord, what a confusion that would make! 'I don't remember,' she said, trying to shrink into invisibility.

'Please step out of the car,' he ordered, very watchful now, the gun in a half-raised position. Stacey was mesmerised by that gun. The hole in the barrel looked to be as big as a cannon, and behind it she could see the dull rounded heads of the bullets in its revolving chamber. Her teeth began to chatter.

'Put your hands on the car and spread your legs,' he instructed. She turned to comply, just as a squealing of brakes announced that another vehicle had stopped near them. She felt one of the officer's hands begin to pat her shoulder and side, when the voice she least wanted to hear in all the world demanded, 'What the hell are you doing to my wife!'

The Ranger was as startled as she was. Out of the corner of her eye she saw him whirl around, gun at the ready, and then stop. 'Mr Marsden?'

'Yes—Harry Marsden. You know me?'

'Yes, sir. I was in the guard of honour at your grand-mother's funeral.'

'Then surely you must know that this little lady is my wife?' Damn them both, Stacey whispered under her breath. Listen to them! The *old boy* network in full swing. This *little lady*—how degrading can they make it sound! Forgive her, officer. She is, after all, only a woman!

'No, I didn't know that,' the Ranger returned, holstering his gun. 'She was in that black veil. And today she claims to be someone else.'

'Ah.' Another nail in my coffin, Stacey thought. The poor little lady is confused! I wish I were ten feet tall, so I could mangle both of them!

'Ah,' Harry repeated. 'Well, you know how it is, officer. We've not been married very long, and we had a—a little misunderstanding. You *do* understand?'

Stacey turned around to face them, a mad glare in her eyes, only to find that they were standing with their backs turned towards her, paying her no attention at all. She swallowed her anger. She was still in a tight spot—

but wait until I get you afterwards, Harry Marsden! she raged to herself.

'Then there's this business about the stolen car,' the Ranger interjected, gesturing back to the jeep.

'Stolen? Why, that's my car,' said Harry. 'I was giving her driving lessons in it.'

'Then you'd better make sure she gets her licence before she goes out on the highway,' the Ranger concluded, shoving his notebook back into its clip. 'She drives like she's following a snake down the road. And at her speed we would have had traffic piled up in back of her all the way to Dallas.'

'Not to worry,' Harry assured him. 'I've got everything in hand. I'll just move the jeep off to the side here, and send someone down to drive it back to the farm. And the little lady—well, I guess I'd better take her with me and reason with her.'

The Ranger tipped him a salute and went back to his patrol car. Harry, completely ignoring Stacey walked over to the jeep and moved it off into the breakdown lane. As he walked back to her his hands were in his pockets, and he was whistling a tune that had no real melody. She turned to face him, red anger showing, her fists clenched so tightly that her nails were biting into her palms. He took one good look.

'Not a good time to say anything, is it?' he suggested diffidently. She tried her best to glare him to death. It brought a smile to the corners of his mouth.

'Would you be willing to climb into my car?' he offered, waving toward the Mercedes. She sniffed at him, and stalked around to the passenger side. He was there before her, holding the door open. Stacey inserted herself without even looking at him. He went around to the driver's seat, started the engine, and turned on the blessed air condition

'We'll go back to the house and talk this over,' he said.

'No!' she shouted at him. 'I've had enough. Take me home!'

He took another close look at her, noting the flushed cheeks, the sparking eyes, and the marks of strain around her mouth. He shrugged his shoulders, and took the car out into the south-bound traffic.

Not another word was said during the whole trip, until the car pulled up into the front yard of the Rancho Miraflores. Stacey's hand went immediately to the door handle, but it refused to open.

'Unlock the door,' she gritted at him.

'No. We have to talk.'

'I don't have anything more to talk about,' she snapped, pushing feebly against the door. 'It was all a farce from beginning to end. I needed you, but you didn't need me. I'm not your wife. I'm not even sure that I like you.'

'What a lie that is, Kitten,' he returned. One of his fingers rummaged through her hair. The contact was more than she could stand. It jolted her, shook her confidence in herself—and made her admit, at least to herself, that what she had said was the biggest lie she had ever told, in all her life. But she had to fight back. That, at least, was something her father had left her: always be prepared to fight back! She shifted away from him on the seat.

'Take your hands off me!' she snarled. 'The game is over. I'm not your wife, I'm not a good enough actress to go on with this lie. Unlock the door and let me out.' Out of the corner of her eye she saw the twins sauntering around the corner of the house, becoming interested spectators.

'And that's another thing,' she snarled. 'Get your cowhands off my ranch, you hear!'

'Oh, I hear all right,' Harry said solemnly. 'You have a remarkably clear voice when you want to, Stacey. And they're not my cowhands. They work for Westland Cattle Associates. You gave me a power of attorney, you'll remember. Rancho Miraflores hired those two young men, and they stay hired until that power of attorney is revoked. Do you want to do that?'

'I—I—' No, I don't want to do that, she cried silently. It's all too much for me. I need you. I hate you, but I need you. And that's not true either. I love you and I need you, but you're going to live in that house with Lisette Langloise for three months, and what chance do I have? 'No, I don't want to cancel.'

'Very well, that's one step in the right direction. Now, how about the rest of it?' Harry leaned in her direction and those two huge hands seized her shoulders and pulled her across the seat, hard up against his warm male frame. 'Now what's the real reason you're blowing your top?'

'I—you and that damn Ranger,' she stormed into his shirt button. 'The little lady. The idiot child—she's only a woman, of course. My God, but you've got a nerve!'

'But it did keep you out of jail, didn't it?'

Stacey snapped her head back to get a clear look at his face. Just one glint of amusement, she promised herself, just one glimmer of a laugh, and I'll—I'll—But his face was solemnity itself, betraying not a quiver or a grin.

'So now suppose you just tell me why you ran away from the house?' suggested Harry.

'You didn't need me any more,' she sobbed. 'You didn't need me at all. It was just a game, and I'm through playing!' To emphasise her point she struggled with the two rings on her left hand, jerking them off at the expense of a little skin. She threw them up on the dashboard in front of him. 'And there's your jewellery. It's all over!'

'You really mean that, Stacey?'

'Oh God, please—just unlock the door and let me go.' The tears were beyond her control and when she raised her face to him she had no idea of the wild appeal it flashed. Harry sighed and shook his head wearily. His fingers went over to the instrument panel and flicked a switch. Stacey heard the snap as the door unlocked, and fought her way across the seat and out on to the baked earth of the yard.

'Kitten!' Harry called after her, but she turned her back and stamped up to the porch, past the two gawking cowboys.

'Doesn't anyone on this ranch have any work to do?' she snarled at them as she slammed into the house and leaned back against the door. Behind her she could hear the whisper of the engine starting up again, and the tyres of the Mercedes squealed as Harry made an angry U-turn. She rushed out into the kitchen, slamming that door behind her too, and then collapsed across the kitchen table, crying her heart out for everything she has lost. Aunt Ellen hurried into the kitchen behind her, flustered. Stacey got up and fled into her arms, and they cried over each other until their tear ducts were empty. Two lonely women.

Stacey wiped her eyes clear with one knuckle. Her hand wandered lightly over her aunt's disfigured cheek. 'You know,' she said determinedly, 'at least that's something we can do something about, Aunt Ellen. Plastic surgery. Think about it!'

As she went up to bed that night in her tiny, draughty room, Stacey thought about it again herself. They had plenty of money. Plastic surgery could give her aunt another face, another chance. I wonder, she thought, just before she closed her eyes, if I could arrange for a heart transplant to give *me* another chance!

CHAPTER SIX

THE week that followed was a succession of bad days. Stacey kept to her room, coming out only for a quick snack in the kitchen, eating because she knew she had to, rather than because she was hungry. Her aunt shadowed her, but did not try to force a confidence. The sun shone almost every day, but there was no real cheer. She wasted box after box of tissues, and thought. At the weekend, still tired and dispirited, she had her answers, and came out into the world. Aunt Ellen was in the kitchen, up to her elbows in flour.

'You're looking better,' her aunt commented.

'Yes,' Stacey replied firmly. 'I have to get a lot of things done. Harry and I—we—' It was too hard to say.

'I know,' her aunt returned. 'I talked to him on the telephone a couple of times this week. He wanted to know how you were.'

'Did he really?' Stacey snapped up the information, not sure whether it made her happy, or just complicated things more. Don't think about Harry just yet, her mind insisted. Get about your business!

'Is Mr Steuben still drilling?' she asked.

'No, I don't think so,' Aunt Ellen responded, after some thought. 'They found water—in seven different places. Another company is working down in the south pasture now, running pipes, setting up pumps, watering troughs—that sort of thing. We've got new water in the house, in case you didn't notice. The old well was getting brackish. You can actually drink this stuff right out of the faucet. And they put in a new automatic pump and a new cistern in the attic. Now all we have to do is turn on the faucet to turn on the pump. Isn't that something?'

'That's nice, dear. What are you making?'

'Bread. Those two young men eat it up faster than I can bake it.'

'Do they eat at the house?'

'No, not really. They cook for themselves. They're living down in the old foreman's cottage. But I do like to contribute. Nice boys, both of them. What are you thinking about? Your face is all screwed up, and you've been wearing a frown all week.'

'What I'm thinking of, Aunt Ellen, is that we two ought to settle down and do something good for ourselves.'

'Do something? What, for example.'

'Well—I learned while I was living at the Marsden house just how little I really know,' Stacey explained. 'I've got to find some way to finish my high school education, and maybe even go to college. But I don't know who to contact, or what to say. And I need a driver's licence, and—' She fumbled to a stop. What use was it to blur out all her secrets? The second greatest want in her life was related to her father, and those crazy helicopters of his. She wanted to fly—to do something to remind herself of Dad. 'But I don't even know where to start,' she concluded mournfully.

Aunt Ellen stopped her to-and-fro rush and looked at Stacey, as if she wanted to say something but dared not. Then she plucked up her courage. 'Why don't you call that nice Miss Moreland?'

'Miss Moreland?' Stacey's mind felt dull, almost as it did when she had been taking all those pills. She shook her head and tried again. 'Do I know a Miss Moreland?'

'Well, you ought to, for goodness' sakes. She's your husband's executive secretary. Amie Moreland. By the way, what happened to your rings?'

'I—we—there was a problem with the fitting, and Harry took them back to the jewellers.' Which was as good a lie as she could concoct in a hurry. Times had changed considerably between her aunt and herself in the past few weeks, but Stacey could not forget that

Harry was the defensive wall behind which she had hidden. And wanted to hide again, if the truth be known. Explanations would be required some time— but if it could all be put off until tomorrow?

'Yes,' her aunt continued, 'last week, after you had that idea, I called Miss Moreland, and within three days she had all the information. A nice girl, that one. Or perhaps I should say woman?'

'I don't know. I've never seen her. What idea was that that I had?'

'Oh dear, surely you haven't forgotten? About the plastic surgeon?' The older woman's upper lip was trembling. Oh Lord, Stacey thought, what have I done now!

'Oh, I remember that very well,' she hurried to say. The lip stilled, and a smile flashed across her aunt's face.

'Well, I thought it over for a time, and it seemed to be such a good idea—so I decided to go ahead. If I can find the money, that is.'

Stacey waved a hand carelessly. One afternoon, just before the funeral, Harry had taken her in to the First National Bank in Waco, and stood laughingly at her side while a vice-president explained to her about the contents of her investment portfolio, and her checking accounts. She had been aware for years that she was 'in oil,' but the size of the quarterly royalty cheque deposited directly into her account by Parsons Oil had taken her breath away. 'Are you sure you've got the decimal point in the right place?' she had asked, in all innocence—and then turned blush-red as half the bank employees within hearing started to laugh. Harry had touched her cheek with one finger, and traced a circle there just before he planted a kiss in its centre. She remembered that now, and her hand came up to caress the spot, still marked in memory.

'Don't worry about the money,' she said. 'There's plenty for everything now. What did you find out?'

'Everything seems to be all arranged, my dear. I'm

sorry I didn't talk it over with you beforehand, but once I called Amie, things just seemed to happen—so fast that I haven't caught my breath yet. I'm to go down to the Texas Medical Centre in Houston very soon. I'll stay there for a week or two, for examinations. Then, if they think anything can be done, I'll go back again. Perhaps around the first of the year—if the money is available. They said, over and above our Blue Cross insurance, perhaps twelve thousand dollars. That's a great deal of money, Stacey.'

'No, it isn't,' she returned, with only half her mind engaged. Miss Moreland, was it? Could it be possible to call her for some advice, without leaning on Harry? Perhaps without him even knowing? Because that was the core of all her dreams. To force-educate herself, to become more sophisticated—to grow older in a hurry. And then go back to Harry and say, 'See, I'm all grown up. Now what?'

And of course Harry would sweep her off her feet, and instantly fall in love with her, and then they would be married, and raise cattle and kids. Perhaps not in that order!

'So you think I should go ahead?' Aunt Ellen was clutching at the edge of the kitchen table as if her life depended on it. Their relationship had completely changed. Where once the older woman had ruled the roost, now she had relinquished all authority, and lived in a half-world between acceptance and rejection. Looking at the unmarred side of her face, Stacey could see her father all over again—the same forehead, the strong nose, the dark grey eyes, all there in his sister's face. And deserving of love, she told herself. Who am I to condemn her for snatching at the golden wedding ring? Look what a fool I'm making of myself about Harry. And if I don't condemn her, then I should show her.

Stacey smiled across the table, walked around it and put her arms around her aunt. 'We're all that's left of the Bronfields,' she said. 'We have to take care of each other. I love you for who you are, my dear. Of course you should go ahead. We've some money in the bank, and there'll be more on the first of October. And while we're at it, let's both run in to Gatesville and buy ourselves a few pretties to wear!'

John Morgan drove them out and back, package-laden. But it was not for another hour after they had returned that Stacey was able to sneak off into the living room and make that all-important telephone call. Amie Moreland turned out to be a delight to talk to, and hard to get to. Her call to the Marsden Management switch-board encountered delays, shifts, re-connections, and a succession of young voices repeating, 'And what would you like to talk to Mrs Moreland about?'

By the time the correct extension was rung, Stacey learned, to the detriment of her confidence, that Amie Moreland was Mrs Moreland, exceedingly busy, executive secretary to the president of the company, a member of the board of directors in her own right, and a very warm-voiced lady who responded cheerfully to Stacey as 'young Mrs Marsden.' Which seemed a very adequate summary of things.

Her explanations were slightly fuzzy, coloured by a stammer she thought she had lost in her childhood. The call lasted forty minutes, during which time the 'very busy' Mrs Moreland asked questions, made notes, and finally said, 'I don't know a single thing about any of this, Mrs Marsden—Stacey. But I do know how to find out. Shall I just go ahead and get things started?'

'If you would—Amie?' Stacey used the name diffidently, having received permission, but not sure that she should. 'I'm in a terrible hurry. I've wasted a great many years, and—' And not for the life of me am I going to tell you *why* I'm in a hurry, or what my ultimate goal is!

'Let me check the list again.' There was a silence. Stacey could hear voices in the background. A few words filtered through. 'It's your wife, Harry. She has a few small problems that—' and then a softer buzz of indistinguishable words. Finally Amie was back at the telephone. 'I think I have everything lined up,' the soft contralto voice said, 'and I don't see why we can't have something going very soon. You'll be at home? Or at the ranch?'

'At the ranch. And I'll be here every day, waiting. Only—Amie—please don't tell—' she was about to say Mr Marsden, until her mind caught up with her tongue— 'Harry?'

'No, of course not.' The woman on the other end of the line giggled. 'What men don't know won't hurt them! I've been married a couple of years myself.'

The smile was still on Stacey's face as she hung up the telephone and walked back into the kitchen.

The next morning, after her first good night's sleep since coming back home, Stacey was up early to face a beautiful sun rising over Beaumont way. After a quick breakfast of toast and coffee she strolled out behind the house for her first real look at what had been done while she was away. Jim Morgan—or was it John?—was squatting down on his heels outside the barn, tinkering with a bridle. He stretched himself up as she came over.

'Ma'am.' He tipped a finger to the brim of his hat in salute. 'This bridle's chewed a fare-thee-well, but I'm fit and determined to stay right here until it's mended.' He smiled down at her with a grin that reminded her of Harry, and it was like a stab in the heart. She turned away from him to hide the tears. He noticed her confusion, and repeated himself. 'Right here until it's mended.' Of course he said it all in that flat Texas drawl that made it come out sounding like 'raght cheer', but Stacey was accustomed to all sorts of accents in cosmopolitan Texas.

'Tell me what's going on,' she prodded him.

'Around these parts, you mean?' She nodded. 'Well, my brother, he's gone into town to get that car you ordered. We done got some help last week, and the corral is all built. The barn is in first-class shape, and some men from Waco are building that wooden-fenced paddock for them Arab horses. Whoeee, ain't they something? And—yeah, we done rode the ranch fence-line, Jim and me, and repaired that. The water is flowing all over the place. And—well now, I sort of forget, we been so busy. Oh yeah, the oil company come in one day last week, they did, and fenced around all them pumps, so the cattle won't be trying to munch on them. And I guess that's all. The boss said we was to get everything ship-shape for spring, 'cause that's when the herd will be coming in. And that's all I know for sure, ma'am. Oh, I did forget—them guys was here to measure the house. And that's it for sure.'

'It—all sounds so very busy,' Stacey commented hesitantly. How in the world does the owner of a spread ask a ranch hand what the devil's going on here? But curiosity outweighed caution. 'They came to measure the house?'

'Well, I don't know about that, ma'am. They was talkin' about making it bigger, and a new roof, and paint—and things like that. That's out of my line.'

'Mine too,' she laughed nervously. He squatted down to his work again, and she joined him, plucking at a blade of grass to nibble on. 'And what car was that, the one your brother went to town for?'

'Oh, that. Well, we drawed straws, you know, right after the boss called. Oh yeah, we got us a telephone down to the cottage now. So anyway, the car's all picked out, over to the car place in Gatesville. He done that himself—the boss did—and Jim, he's got nothin' to do all this week but teach you how to drive it, and help you get your licence.'

All of which was plenty to think about as she rode her mare around the perimeter of the ranch, admiring the neat fencing, and the return of green to the landscape after the storm which had broken the back of the drought. The long flat vista stretched out all around her, broken only by clumps of cottonwood trees. In the

western distance the hills loomed, outlining the valley of
the Lampassas River, but beyond the boundaries of the
ranch. Everything in sight seemed to be imbued with
new life, new promise. And the only pain in her heart
came from the thought that her father could not be there
to see it.

It took more than the week before Jim Morgan was
satisfied with her performance at the wheel. The car he
had brought proudly back was an American Eagle, a
four-wheel-drive station wagon, heavily sprung to match
the needs of ranch driving. When she finally met his
requirements, he took her down to the warehouse dis-
trict of the huge military post, Fort Hood, where
examiners had previously arranged for the testing of
several Army officers from other states.

Stacey breezed through the written examination, then
went out for the road test. There was just a moment of
nervousness as she watched the big husky Ranger come
over towards where she was parked. 'If it's him, I'll fall
through the floor,' she mumbled to herself. But when
the officer arrived, he was not the same man who had
stopped her on that wild day on Route 35! She stalled the
engine immediately, and the Ranger laughed.

'Par for the course,' he chuckled. 'Don't be so nervous, Mrs Marsden.' And that was enough to take the
edge off. She sailed through the parking manoeuvres,
the passing test, and the road run. 'And you pass with
flying colours,' the officer said. 'Now be sure, always
carry your licence with you when you drive!'

Her face was blush-red when they handed her the
permit. She had been on a high jag of excitement until
that moment, but with the permit in hand, exhaustion hit
her so hard she had not the strength to drive them both
back to the Ranch. It was the first of her goals accomplished. She checked it off in her mind and wondered
when she might start on the next.

Two days later she found out. It was almost as if
someone off-stage had been waiting for her to get her

licence before turning to the next page of the script. She had awakened happily, bent on going out immediately and driving somewhere—anywhere. Aunt Ellen was in the kitchen, smiling to herself as she put together a real Texas breakfast.

'Steak and eggs?' enquired Stacey, peering over her shoulder.

'Just so,' her aunt returned. 'I heard from Jim—or was it John?—that you did real well yesterday. You deserve a real breakfast.'

'And I'm ready for it,' Stacey laughed as she set the kitchen table for two. 'But why are you so happy? Not because I got my licence, surely?'

'No, not exactly.' Her aunt still wore that secret smile, that expression that lit up the inner woman. 'I talked to Mrs Moreland again yesterday, and she says the doctors are ready for me, beginning next Wednesday.' She hugged herself, trying to contain her glee. 'Oh, Stacey,' she sighed, 'you'll never know how much this means to me, and after all I did to hurt you!' The glow produced tears. Stacey hurried over and hugged her. The minute her arms went around the older woman, she knew what she herself had been missing all these days—two warm comforting arms, and the pleasure of touching! They sat down opposite each other at the breakfast table, having cemented one more brick into the structure of their family relations.

Stacey did the dishes while her aunt wandered off in a happy daze. The vacuum cleaner began to hum at about the same time that the doorbell rang. Stacey dried her hands and walked to the front door. It had been so long since anyone had used that door that she could hardly remember the occasion. Everyone came to the side door, in typical farm fashion. An elderly man, barely five and a half feet tall, with white hair and a stringy Vandyck beard, stood waiting.

'Bob Herndon,' he introduced himself. 'Will you tell your mother that I'm here?'

'My mother?'

'Yes—Mrs Marsden. That is your mother, isn't it?'

Stacey looked down at her denim-clad figure, almost completely covered by a huge kitchen apron—the one with the crimson letters that said 'Texas Beef Barbecues Best,' her hair combed back under a kerchief that left her looking twelve years old, and laughed. He joined her, obviously not knowing why. 'Come in,' Stacey giggled, and gestured him into the front parlour. He walked by her, juggling his briefcase from one hand to the other to accommodate his cane.

'Old age,' he apologised as her eye swung to the cane. 'Old age, and—er—fast living, perhaps.' He sank down into one of the overstuffed chairs without waiting for an invitation. 'Your mother?'

'Oh, yes, my mother. I think there's some mistake,' she told him slowly. 'My mother has been dead for many years. I'm Mrs Marsden.'

'You? Why—' his urbane manner disappeared in the confusion, and then he laughed again, 'of course, Mrs Marsden. I've been sent by Federal Electronics.' Stacey snapped to attention. Federal Electronics—that *other* company that rented space in the Marsden Management business! 'I'm a retired schoolteacher, to be exact. I and a small group of other retired teachers have banded together in a company called Tutorials, Inc. We specialise in High School Equivalency Testing.'

'Do you really?' Her mind was on other things. For example, what business was it of Federal Electronics to send someone to *her* door? 'What in the world is that?'

'Many states, including Texas,' he explained, 'recognise that a considerable number of adults who didn't finish their high school courses would like to have a diploma. So the Equivalency Test was established. Very simply, if you take the test and pass, the State of Texas will award you a high school diploma. There are no strings attached.'

'But I—I haven't been in school for years,' Stacey protested. 'I don't think I could pass *any* kind of test.'

'Not to worry,' he told her. 'That's what I'm here for—to serve as tutor for you in any weak subjects you might have, and to see that you *do* pass the test. So sure are we in our guarantee that we don't charge a fee until you've successfully taken the examination. Shall we begin?'

And begin they did. First with a diagnostic test that painfully indicated Stacey's need of tutoring in math and Social studies, and then with intensive drills and tutoring, every morning except Saturday and Sunday, until her brain cried out against further stuffing. Stacey kept her nose to the grindstone as the cycle of the year rolled down.

Every afternoon she spent two hours or more with her studies, then saddled her old mare for a brief ride through the changing ranchland.

Suddenly summer had gone. She marked it well. From time to time friends of her father came to adjacent Fort Hood, and came out to the ranch to reminisce. More often than not, in the heat of the season, they would invite her back to the fort to use the outdoor pool at the Officers' Club. And summer's end was announced on October the fifteenth, when the unheated pool was closed for the winter.

During that same month Aunt Ellen went off to Houston for her diagnostic tests. Stacey had planned all along to drive her to Waco Airport to flaunt her seldom-used driver's licence. But that unseen hand that manipulated her life was before her again. When she judged it time to leave for the airport her aunt gave her one of those big smiles, and refused to budge. An hour later a clatter in the sky announced the arrival of a helicopter. Stacey went out on the porch, slipping on a light sweater against the cool wind, and watched the whirly-bird set down behind the house. It was one of those big Sikorsky heavy-duty jet jobs, all blue and white, with WEST-

LAND CATTLE painted in garish red on one side. The pilot was Jim Morgan—or perhaps John.

He climbed down out of the cockpit and came over to her, ducking under the threat of the rotating blades, even though they were ten feet or more above his head.

'I didn't know you were a helicopter pilot,' she yelled in his ear.

'Am I?' he asked, equally loud. 'Oh, that, you mean. Yes, I am. Jim too, for that matter. Is your aunt ready?'

'Yes, she'll be out in a minute. The—other one of you is getting her bags together now.' She swung both hands behind her back and crossed all available fingers. 'I wish I could fly one of those things.'

'It takes a mite of doin',' he advised, being just as casual about it as she was. 'Nigh on to a hundred hours of just ground instruction, you know.' Aunt Ellen came out the door, struggling against the backlash of the helicopter-created wind, and Stacey knew she had very little time to pin down a commitment.

'But you could teach me if you wanted to?' She found it difficult to be coy and little-girlish when she had to shout at the top of her lungs. And in any event, Morgan was having none of it.

'You got one or two words wrong,' he yelled in her ear. 'I could teach you if *he* wanted to.'

'Who are you talking about?'

'The boss man. I work for Westland Cattle. If the boss says teach you, I teach you. If the boss says no, I don't. Makes life simple, ma'am. I gotta run now.' And he suited action to words.

Stacey gave her aunt a parting hug, wished her well, then stood back as the chopper took off in another swirl of dust, circled once, and headed eastward. And while she watched, her mind ran around the outside of the problem, trying to find a hole leading into the central core of it. Who was responsible for all this? Amie Moreland? Or somebody she hadn't even met yet? Who, for example, was the head man of the cattle company? That might be a good place to start, but right this minute, as the sounds of the helicopter faded in the distance, she knew that more immediate problems must be faced. Her tutor, Mr Herndon, had agreed to come in the afternoon on this one day, and she had yet to complete the three pages of algebraic equations he had assigned from the day before. She waved at Jim Morgan, in the distance, who was headed for the corral with a saddle slung over his shoulder, and for just a minute entertained a rebellion against her own rules—but quickly passed it up. Her goal was still too distant, and no minutes could be squandered on the road leading there.

The days trudged after each other, one on one, like a herd of elephants in a single line, none different from another, all plodding, driving, skull-shattering. 'Your history is good,' Mr Herndon had told her, 'and so is your English. But there has to be more drill in Maths, and your Spanish is atrocious. Dig in, girl!' And she did.

Aunt Ellen arrived back at the ranch after a two-week absence, happy, with an affirmative report from the doctors. 'They want to start skin grafts right after the first of the year,' she told her niece. 'They say it may take as much as three separate operations, over a period of three or four months.'

'Do you want it to happen?' asked Stacey.

'Indeed I do,' her aunt chortled. 'They had an artist come in, and he drew me a picture of how it would look when they finish! Oh yes, I want it to happen!' The glow that she brought into the house was enough to last for the remainder of the week.

After Stacey had done her lessons, earning her a grudging 'not bad' from her tutor, she wandered outside. The helicopter was still there, sitting like an ugly duck in a little depression behind the house. One of the Morgan brothers came out of the barn as soon as Stacey approached the machine.

'I talked to the boss man,' he said laconically. 'He

says, give the little lady anything she wants. When you wanna start?'

'How about right now?' she returned eagerly. 'I'm free every afternoon.'

'Takes a heap of studying,' he said. 'And you ain't exactly unemployed right now. You sure?'

She was sure, but a little disappointed to find out that the first hundred hours were practically all theory—communications, navigation, and a dozen other topics, with only a few familiarisation rides in the machine to keep up her enthusiasm. But thoughts of her father drove her—of her father, and Harry. And of the goals she had set for herself.

November passed into December. The Thanksgiving turkey was shared by herself, her aunt, and the two ranch hands. A trip down to Pidcoke to say her thanks in the church in which she had been baptised, then back deep into the books again.

The weather changed in December. The arctic winds began to roar down the Mississippi valley from Canada, straight into the Texas panhandle, then farther down, to the valley of the Brazos. There was a little snow, and on December the twentieth, when as much as half an inch fell, practically all of Coryelle County seemed to come to a standstill under the unusual threat.

On December the twenty-second Stacey drove herself proudly into Gatesville and sat for her examination. She had gone in demurely dressed, hair carefully brushed, cheeks shining with expectation. She came out bedraggled, tired, drained, surrounded by a dozen or more other adults who had come for the same purpose. They were all in need of conversation. She was so sure that she had made an unholy mess of the affair that she slunk away, backed her Eagle out of the parking area, and had driven home like a madwoman, wondering what she could turn to next.

Christmas was a quiet time. One of the men had cut a small fir tree for them, and the two women set it up in the living room, decorating it with wildly improbable baubles they had picked up at a sale in Killeen. It looked incongruously like a tiny burro trying to bear the load designed for a mule. They had a quiet laugh for themselves, opened two bottles of Lone Star beer in honour of the occasion, and went off to bed.

The Morgan boys went home for Christmas Day, leaving the women alone. They both slept late, and barely made it to church services. When they came back they found a cruiser from the Sheriff's patrol waiting for them at the door.

'Just a check-up, ladies,' the young Deputy told them. 'We've got orders to keep an eye open for you over the holidays.'

'Does that mean you know something about the Delanos?' Stacey hated to raise the spectre, but could not hold back.

'Nope,' he replied. 'Them two is long gone—north, I suspect. The young one was seen in Chicago a few weeks ago, but got away. Don't you worry none. We'll be keeping a close watch. Merry Christmas!'

They wandered into the house after exchanging greetings. As usual, the side door had been left open, and Stacey knew that someone had been there in her absence. There was a smell of cigar smoke in the air, and an additional present under the tree.

Under the layers of wrapping and packing tissue was a glass box, about twenty inches high, and four to six inches deep. Stacey fumbled eagerly with the wrappings, and managed to get the box out. Inside the glass case, sealed in some preservative, were two long-stemmed roses, intertwined. A key was set into the base of the box. She turned it a couple of times, and began to cry as the music box inside stumbled through 'I Love You Truly'. There was no card.

For the rest of the day she carried the case around with her, treasured in the crook of her arm. Occasionally she turned the key a few twists, just enough to get the first few bars of the old love song. Aunt Ellen kept to the kitchen, humming to herself as she heard the echo of the music box sounding from all over the house. Stacey took it to bed with her, nestling it on the empty pillow next to her own. At two o'clock in the morning she awoke to moonlight, and stood by the window looking eastward, clutching the encased roses in her hands.

But it was back to work the day after Christmas. She did not expect to see her tutor again until after the New Year, but she felt so badly about the exam that she pulled out all her reference books and buried herself in the work. The only interruption was the sound of the mailman's horn, as he announced a deliver at the roadside box.

'Somebody's got some mail,' Aunt Ellen called out to her.

'I heard,' she said wistfully. 'For you, I suppose. I'll go and get it—I need the air.' She struggled into the old sheepskin coat that hung by the side door. It's getting a bit straggly, she noted. And why not? You've had it for four years, girl. How about that? Six months ago she never would have noticed. Now she did.

A blast of frigid air slapped her in the face as she stepped down off the porch and headed for the mailbox. From the barn she could tell from the noise that the Morgans were back. Animals have to eat, no matter what the human holiday. A thin wisp of smoke shot up from the chimney of the house, to be instantly seized by the wind and torn to shreds. Stacey pulled her coat collar up tighter, and headed down the track.

There were four letters and two newspapers in the Rural Delivery box. Stacey crammed them into the capacious pockets of her coat and hurried back to the house. The wind was already finding the leaks between the loose buttons.

That same wind snatched the door from her hands as she came back up the steps, slamming it back against the doorstop with a thud. 'You've got some mail,' she called out as she dropped the envelopes on the table, shed her coat, and went back to deal with the door, two-handed.

Aunt Ellen brought in a mug of steaming coffee, and she accepted it gladly, using the heat from the mug to warm her hands. She sipped gently at it, daydreaming. Her aunt handed her an envelope. 'This one's for you,' she said.

The envelope had a return address on it: 'School Department, Coryelle County.' Stacey almost dropped the cup of coffee in her eagerness to open the letter. Tangled fingers tore at the seal and, after much fumbling, managed to extract the thin single-page letter.

'We are pleased to inform you,' the letter said briefly, 'that you have passed the High School Equivalency Test with a score of 97.8%. A certificate and a diploma will be mailed to you in due course.'

Which meant after New Year, she told herself. Passed! After all that sweat and tears! Passed! She could not hold back. She flashed the letter under her aunt's nose, shrieked a couple of times in glee, and went over to the corner where all her books and work papers were settled. 'No more!' she shouted at them, and hurled everything up in the air, to fall where it would. 'I did it!'

'You did indeed!' Her aunt came over to join her, and the two of them danced together wildly around the room, until sheer exhaustion forced the older woman to call a halt. 'If I ever get my breath back,' Aunt Ellen threatened, 'we'll have a celebration. I can make a cake, and—'

The telephone interrupted. It had stood silent for so many days that they were both startled. Stacey hesitantly picked it up and offered a tentative 'hello'.

'Stacey, this is Amie Moreland.' She knew who it was before the name was announced; it was that kind of voice. 'I understand that you heard from the school department?'

'Why, I—just this minute,' Stacey stammered. 'How in the world did you know?'

'Oh, I have spies everywhere,' the woman chuckled. 'Did you get a good mark?'

'I guess I did. I know I did! 97.8%! I think that's pretty high. And I want to thank you for all your trouble. Everything worked so nicely, and Mr Herndon was a real doll, and I wish you would send me the bill.'

'I think it's already been paid,' said Amie. 'Out of your investment portfolio, or something. Well now, with that out of the way, are you prepared to go on? I mean with the plan you suggested?'

'Yes, more than ever. I suppose there's a waiting period—until next fall, perhaps?'

'No, I don't think so,' Amie returned. 'I talked to the Dean of Admissions at Baylor University, and he agrees that you could be accepted in probationary status, beginning in the spring term. It starts on January tenth. Too soon?'

'I—no. Wait just a minute, please.' Stacey covered the mouth of the telephone. 'Aunt Ellen, what's the date you have to go back to Houston?'

'On the sixth of January, dear. Does that make a problem?'

'No, not at all,' she answered, and returned to the telephone. 'That would be fine, Amie. What do I have to do?'

'On the seventh—that's a Friday—I want you to come to my office. By about nine o'clock, let's say. There'll be a young man here to guide you through the registration. And, Stacey, you'd better plan to stay in Waco during the week, and go home at the weekends. Is that satisfactory?'

'You mean you've already found me a place to stay?'

'Not exactly, dear. The dormitories are already filled to overflowing. But I can't believe that somewhere in this city of a hundred thousand people we can't find room for one girl student. Is that all right?'

'I—I think it's a minor miracle,' Stacey returned. 'I feel as if I'd found a fairy godmother, or something. I do thank you, Mrs Moreland—Amie—With all my heart. I'll be in your office by nine o'clock on the seventh. And thank you again.'

She hung up the receiver and went around for the rest of the day in a state of shock, treasuring her roses. On her way to bed that night, her ears filled with her aunt's congratulations, she changed into a warm flannel night-gown, and stood barefoot in front of the window, tracing star-patterns. You've taken the first two steps, she told herself. And maybe an inch or two more. You've studied, and been rewarded. You ought to be the happiest girl in the world. You should be sitting on top of Cloud Nine, singing two-part harmony with Stevie Nelson. Yes, you should!

She walked over to the bed and sat down on it, feeling the fingers of a dull headache reaching out for her. Yes, I should be the happiest girl in the world, she assured herself, through the dull throbbing pain. So how come I wake up every night, crying?

CHAPTER SEVEN

HER first three weeks as a university coed went by so quickly that Stacey had no time to assess her situation. And she learned a great deal in those weeks. She met Amie Moreland, a roly-poly raven-haired woman of about thirty. 'Before I married I was a Lopez,' she explained, laughing. 'And my husband is of Norwegian descent. If all the children turn out to be blue-eyed blonds my mother will kill me! Are you settled in now?'

Settled in? That was a very large question. As predicted, there had been no rooms available in the dormitories, and nothing 'suitable' within two square miles. 'So, since Harry is in Europe, and that whole penthouse apartment is sitting there empty, you might as well move in.'

She did so hesitantly, not working up the nerve to unpack her bags until the end of the second week. It was convenient, being only a few blocks from the campus, and it provided parking space for her car, and a uniformed guard at the entrance. But that big revolving waterbed carried too many memories with it. For the first week she hardly slept at all, lying back in the bed and letting it rotate across the Waco skyline all night long, until the swishing of the liquid soothed her to sleep.

She found it difficult to make friends at school. All the boys seemed too young, and all the girls were babblers. She was of their age, but not of their generation. Harry had spoiled all that for her. So she stuck her nose in the books, and came out only on Thursdays and weekends. The classes themselves were simple, a typical Freshman college curriculum: History, English, Spanish, Economics, and Accounting. But she found a tremendous problem disciplining herself to the school routines. After all, for more than four years she had been away from such things, on her own, and it was difficult to adjust.

At weekends she found the helicopter available to her, sitting on the pad by the building, with either Jim or John Morgan at the controls. They used the ride to Houston as a continuation of her flying lessons. She had already completed the ground instruction, and was well into flight training.

At the hospital, she found that her aunt was recovering slowly from her first operation, but was in good spirits. She spent all of Saturday there, getting the little odds and ends her aunt wanted, cheering her up, and taking voluminous orders about things to be done at home—which never were finished.

Then it was back to Waco late Saturday night. Sunday was her day of rest. She hardly felt the need of study time; her classes met on Monday, Wednesday, and Friday, with one odd two-hour meeting on Tuesday, and nothing on Thursday. After three months under Mr Herndon's whip, she found the college requirements fairly simple.

So on her day of rest she washed clothes, pottered around, went to church, toured some of Waco's entertainment spots, and thought about Harry. It was almost impossible not to, surrounded as she was by his work, his clothing, his books—everything. That last Sunday night, the first week of February, she ate a TV dinner, took a long bath in the hot tub, and then, physically exhausted, went to bed and fell asleep almost at once.

It was one of those typical Texas winter nights. The moon looked in coldly from the west, and a line of high clouds was edging in from the north. The temperature hovered around the freezing mark, and the wind blew hard.

About two in the morning a noise wakened her. It was

the sort of indeterminable noise that one normally puts down to the wind, or a loose shutter. Stacey smiled at her alarm, turned over and started to drift back to sleep, when it struck her. A loose shutter in a penthouse? Come on now, Stacey! Both eyes snapped open, and she turned over on her back, searching the semi-darkness at the head of the stairs. There definitely was a noise.

Footsteps, thumping wearily upward from the apartment below! That's all I need to make my day, she thought—burglars in the middle of the night. It was a tough neighbourhood, trapped between the railroad tracks and the elevated highway, but surely with the guard downstairs—?

She watched, mesmerised, as the footsteps gained a shadow. An arm reached around the corner and snapped the switch that slowly turned the windows from transparent to opaque. Unconsciously she squashed herself up against the head of the bed, knees driven hard into her stomach. Panic rose to engulf her, blocking her throat, straining her breathing. She clasped her arms tightly around her knees, and sat there, shivering.

The shadowy arm moved again, this time to the light switch. The lights came up softly, as if the control knob had barely been turned. Her squeak of recognition alerted the man, and turned him in her direction.

'My God!' he roared. 'So this is where you've been hiding!'

Stacey wanted to roar back at him—to roar and rant and rave, and tell him a few home truths. But nothing came out, except for a weak moan which even she could not recognise. And while her dazed mind tried to re-group its scattered senses, her fool body took command. She bounced off the bed and ran at him, smashing deep into the comfort of his arms.

Frantically she pressed closer, trying to be absorbed in him. Her arms snaked up around his neck, and she pulled herself up on to her toes. His shirt, under the unbuttoned gold of his jacket, was soaking up all the tears. Dry sobs hacked at her throat.

'There now, little lady,' he crooned into the tangled mass of her hair. 'There there now, love—I didn't mean to frighten you half to death.'

One of his hands came up and toyed with her soft golden crown, fingering it like a comb, comforting. Gradually the sobs faded and the tears stopped, replaced by hiccups. He bent slightly and swept one arm under her knees, picking her up and cradling her against his chest as he stalked over to the bed and sat down there, with her shivering body resting on his knees.

'I didn't mean to scare you so,' he repeated.

'You didn't scare me that much,' she managed to get out. 'It's just—oh, Harry, I've missed you so! I thought you'd forgotten me. And after the awful things I said, I couldn't blame you. Oh, Harry!' She nuzzled her face into his shirt again, trying to avoid the searching look in those dark eyes.

He pried her loose, forcing her head back so he could examine her face. One of his huge knuckles came gently up under each eye in succession, and wiped away the last hanging tear. 'There now,' he comforted. 'I could never forget you, Stacey, never.' He pulled her head against his chest again, resting that firm chin on top of her wild hair. 'Better now?'

'I—yes,' she managed weakly. 'I didn't mean to usurp your apartment, but Amie said—'

'Ah—Amie said! Now there's a woman with a lot of explaining to do! Where the devil is she?'

'Amie? Why, she's on vacation. She and Karl went down to Brownsville. She said something about fishing. Karl loves fishing.'

'Yes. And Amie hates it.'

'Well, she said it was his vacation and they were going fishing, and besides, you're in Europe, and nobody has heard a word about when you're coming back, and—but you *are* back, aren't you?' Damn the man, she sighed to herself as she bit down on her tongue. Of course he's back. Why is it that whenever I see him I react like a ten-year-old moron? Babbling! Diarrhoea of the mouth, her father used to say, teasing her. And no wonder he thinks I'm too young for him!

'Yes, I'm back,' he chuckled. 'In fact, I've been back for a week or so.'

'For a week?' Indignation set in. 'And just what the devil have you been doing, not telling anybody!'

'Hey, whoa! I'll tell you what I've been doing, you teasing little minx. I've been looking for you so I could tell you that I'm back. What a run-around you've given me, lady!'

Minx? Teasing? It suddenly came to her that she was dressed only in her nightgown. But it's a warm flannel, she told herself. It covers from neck to ankles, loosely. What the devil does he mean—tease? His free hand came up and perched a finger on the end of her nose, running slowly down across her parted lips, over her chin, into the valley between her half-exposed breasts, where she had failed to fasten any of the six buttons that formed her security guard.

'Oh my!' Her squeak of alarm brought a laugh from him, and cured her hiccups. Her frantic fingers swarmed to her defence, fumbling at the tiny ivory buttons without success.

'Here, let me help.' There was a dollop of sarcasm behind the words. One of his hands imprisoned both of hers, pulling them down into her lap. His other hand, coming completely around her, fumbled with the buttons, inhibited by the wrong angle, but still doing better than *she* had—but not without an occasional brush against the smooth softness of her breasts. Each little touch set her on fire, and she revelled in the feelings, admonishing herself that it was only by casual accident—until she became aware that no more buttons were being closed. Harry's hand had slipped under the yoke of her gown, and was claiming a hardened bronze peak as his prize. Lightning struck at her, a roiling feeling she had never felt before, starting at the captured fortress of her breast and running down into the pit of her being. Vague feelings of alarm were discarded, sent back into the limbo from which they had sprung. His fingers played lightly across her swollen breasts, teasing each one of them in turn.

She felt the coolness as one corner of her gown slipped off a shoulder, to be followed quickly by the other. Now both his hands roved free across her stomach and back, moving in gentle circles from her lips to her breasts, to the tips of her ears. And through it all she trembled more and more as the excitement fed on itself. She had difficulty breathing. Her lungs were no longer able to fill and expand.

She opened her mouth to complain, only to find he had been waiting for the opportunity. His lips came down on hers in the slow gentle movement of a giant wine-press, tantalising at first, then sealing her off from all the outside world. He tasted the honey of her, and strove for more.

Stacey gave herself up to the moment. The searing excitement heated, cooled, and reheated. It was something she had never thought of before, something for which she had never been prepared. This driving passion that demanded she make a gift of herself. A gift of herself? The thought was sobering. Her lips were still sealed by his, but she could feel some movement as one of his hands began to inch the hem of her gown up above her knees and across her thighs—and reason, regrettable reason, intervened.

'No!' she commanded softly as she struggled away from his relentless lips. She pushed herself away, bouncing as the water-bed responded. There was a dazed expression on his face as his hands continued their exploration, and then the stern craggy look returned, his hands made tender farewells. He took a deep breath, lifted her off his lap, and dumped her on the bed.

'No, of course not.' His voice was gruff and strained, as if stopping had taken more energy than he had to give. 'No, I'm sorry—I should have said it first.'

Stacey struggled with her buttons, then moved a few feet farther down the bed, her shaking hands moving to her disarrayed hair, using it to hide her face.

'You don't need to apologise,' she said, with a quiver in her voice. 'It was as much my fault as yours.'

'Don't be a fool,' he snapped. 'You're only eighteen!'

'Still the same old story, huh?' She glowered at him, biting on her lower lip to keep it from trembling. 'Just a kid? Did you know that my mother was seventeen when she married, and only eighteen when I was born? Did you know that?'

'No, I didn't.' His face was losing that fixed determined stare. There was even a tiny glint of humour in his eyes. 'No, I didn't know that, and you're not your mother. Let's get away from this damn bed. I need to talk to you.' He stood up and headed for the stairs leading down to the apartment proper. She watched him move—glide would be more like it. At least he's not mad at me—for the moment! She grabbed her old green robe, shrugging her way into it as she followed behind him. But the time she caught up he was in the kitchen, heating water for instant coffee.

He gestured her into the overstuffed chair on the other side of the coffee table, and sank on to the big couch. She did her best to look adult, brushing her hair away from her face, teasing it with her fingers until it fell in orderly waves down around her shoulders. He sipped once at the too-hot coffee, set the mug down on the low table, and looked at her.

'Well, I found her,' he started out.

'Found who?' I don't want to admit an interest, she told herself fiercely. Why should I make it easy for some—good lord, she must be thirty or more—for some old bitch to take my place!

'Lisette,' he said slowly. 'Lisette Langloise, my grandmother's godchild. You surely remember her?'

'Oh, vaguely,' she muttered. That's all I needed, just a little more time. Just enough for him to see that I'm not a child. Just a reasonable time for me to improve myself, to become more sophisticated! That had been the subject of her prayers for the last three months, just before she dropped off to sleep. Let him find her, Lord, but not right away. Give me time, Lord. Let him wait for me!

'Yes, I remember now. It was something about the will, wasn't it?'

'Oh, come on, Stacey.' He was laughing at her again, or at least his eyes were. 'You remember every single thing about it, don't you?' It wasn't really a question, it was a command.

'Yes,' she sighed, 'everything. Tell me what happens next?'

'So I brought her home. I found her in Paris, trying to live the good life. And someone else, too—I'll tell you about that later. Lisette is sick—a stupid thing. She says she has tuberculosis, but she won't let me call in a doctor. When I caught up with her she was in a hospital in the eighth Arrondissement. A charity patient, would you believe that!'

And that really pops my cork, Stacey sighed to herself. Had the woman come home beautiful, rich, poor, interesting—any of them I could have put up a fight against. But instead she had come home sick. He wouldn't turn a sick dog away—and now the beautiful Lisette Langloise would really get her hooks into him!

'She looks like death warmed over,' Harry continued, musingly. The statement caught Stacey flatfooted. All her wild dreams had been about that moment of confrontation, when the gloriously beautiful Lisette was completely outfaced by the young but sophisticated Stacey Bronfield. She looks like death warmed over? I don't know whether to laugh or cry! So she did neither.

'That's too bad,' she muttered, not too convincingly.

'Don't overwhelm me with your grief,' he said sarcastically. 'The girl is really sick.' And how about *that*! Stacey told herself. Thirty years old, and still a *girl*. But also, no matter how much she wanted to, Stacey was unable to wish her opponent more suffering.

'I did mean it,' she said, somewhat more convincingly. 'What can I do to help?'

'I knew you'd say that!' he exulted. 'I hate to keep coming back to you, but I need you again. I need you badly.'

'Yes—well—' Almost she blurted out *and I need you too, Harry. Need you badly. I ache all over, from teeth to toenails, from the needing you.* 'Tell me what you want me to do.'

'I don't know how to say it,' he muttered, reaching across the table to snatch up her hand. 'She's—different, changed a lot from what she once was. That bastard she married cut her loose—divorced her—in Germany, and left her without a penny. She's had to hold her own without any help, and it's made her—well, hard is the word that fits, I guess. Last week when I brought her back to the house it took no more than two days for Millie Fallon to tell me she would rather quit than work for that woman. And the only thing that kept Frank from packing it in was that he was away most of the time, moving my remuda of Arabs.'

'But sick people generally are hard to get along with,' Stacey told him. 'I'm sure Millie will make adjustments. Surely you don't want me to come out there and be your housekeeper?'

'But that's exactly what I do want,' he said. For the first time that night his smile sprawled wide across his face. 'With you in charge, there would be no doubt about who Millie was working for.'

'Come on now,' she retorted. 'Look, it's three-thirty in the morning, and this girl has to be at work by eight-fifteen. Lay it on the line, Harry. You know darn well you could hire a dozen competent housekeepers, and ten thousand nurses, if you wanted them. Just what—'

'What the devil do you mean, *you have to go to work*? Has that damned accountant screwed up again? I'll kill that guy! What's happened!' It had taken only microseconds for the smile to disappear, to be replaced by a glaring rage. I don't know what accountant we're talking about, Stacey told herself, but he'd better buy a ticket to some faraway place, quickly. Harry looked as if he really *could* kill!

'No, it isn't whatever you're thinking,' she snapped at him. 'I don't mean I had to go to work to earn a living. I mean I—well, didn't Amie tell you?'

'Didn't Amie tell me what?' he roared again. She put both hands over her ears and ducked.

'Didn't she tell me what?' he repeated, at about forty decibels lower.

'I—I'm going to school,' she stammered tentatively, and stopped to see if the tornado was about to strike again. He seemed calm—well, almost calm. A corner of his mouth was still twitching, and there was more red showing on his cheeks than she cared for. She tried one more step. 'I—finished High School, and now I'm a freshman probationary student at Baylor.' And then she ducked back out of the way. No explosion. In fact the news sent him back against the sofa, relaxed, and the smile returned.

'You're a co-ed?' he chuckled. 'Stacey?' She nodded. 'You can start breathing again,' he added. 'You're turning blue. I like the idea—grand!'

'Well,' she amended, 'it's only a trial, that's all. If I do well by May, then the Faculty Board will evaluate me, and—' Once again caution caught up with her. She was just about to mention that in May also she would be up for her pilot's licence, providing she could get another six hours of flight time in a fixed wing aircraft.

'Well, I'll be double-dyed and dipped in sheep grease!' It was very definitely a grin again, as big and as broad as the Panhandle. 'I'm proud of you, lady.'

'That's nice,' she said, trying to restrain her own glee. 'Now tell me why you can't just hire a housekeeper, since I'm not available—except on weekends, and on Thursday.'

'That's just fine,' he told her, 'just fine. The house is near enough for you to commute with me in the mornings, and—'

'And that's stalling,' she interrupted, wondering as she did so where she had got the nerve. 'So just flat—out tell me what the score is, please.'

'The score? Oh yes, the score.' Somehow Harry had discovered something very interesting on the floor between them. His eyes refused contact, and she felt the insane urge to reach over, as he had done so often, to tilt up his chin and make him confront her.

'Well, the problem isn't so simple,' he told the rug. 'Lisette had a few days to think things over before we came home, and now she evidently thinks that both the house and I were left to her in the will. And that's something I don't want to encourage. Look, Stacey—I know it's beginning to sound old hat to you, but I need the protection of a wife in the house again!'

'Oh no! Not that!' He looked up at her. His face was masked with a hangdog *I wish she would* look, while her fierce stare did its best to carve him up into tiny pieces. Then there was a twitching at the corners of both mouths, and they simultaneously broke out into laughter. At least Harry did. Stacey was caught in the middle of a wild rage of giggles by another massive hiccup, which entirely routed the solemnity. There were giggle-tears in her eyes when she finally was able to settle down again.

'It's four o'clock now,' she told him, in her best James Bond imitation. 'Synchronise watches. What's our cover story?'

'You read too much of the Fleming stuff,' he chuckled. 'Well, I think something simple. Millie and

Frank have kept asking for you, and I've been telling them that you had to go to Houston to be near your aunt.'

'Oh, you knew about that, did you?' she snapped, her eyes flashing again.

'Yes, I knew about that,' he returned. 'Cool off, banty hen. I arranged it. Your aunt and I have talked two or three times a week for the last four months. Strange she didn't tell me about your school, though. Well, it's not important. Here's our cover story. You had to be with your aunt last week—there were complications, or something. And you're coming directly back to Waco on Monday. I mean today—and then after school you're meeting me here at the office, and away we go. You're a *bona fide* student, God's in his heaven—and why don't we go get a couple of hours of shut-eye before we both have to get to work.'

They both stood up, and Harry opened his arms invitingly. Stacey accepted immediately, leaning against his shirt again, surrounding herself in the comforting warmth of him. 'Your wife shouldn't let you go out with a wet shirt on,' she murmured softly.

'What?'

'I said you just remember that I'm only a rental bride, not the real thing, Harry Marsden.'

'You mean I'm supposed to keep out of your bed?'

'That, and—and you're not to try to seduce me, whether it's in my bed or not. Right?'

'That's a hard bargain you drive,' he said solemnly, and she leaned back to see if that sardonic gleam was in his eye. It was.

CHAPTER EIGHT

A COOL shower helped Stacey pry open her eyes in the morning, and killed her predilection to linger. The alarm clock had failed to go off; it was seven-forty-five in the morning. Harry was still asleep in the waterbed, behind that stupid barrier of pillows that had 'protected' her from him all through the early hours. Ha! Protect indeed. How can you shut off your mind when he's lying there, not two feet away? She had tossed and turned all the remainder of the night, and cursed him heartily for being able to sleep so peacefully.

She slipped into the typical college uniform—worn blue jeans, a bulky sweater, and loafers. A quick brushing re-established order to her hair. She neglected everything else, stopping only to brush her teeth and steal a quick lingering look at Harry, and then dashed for the elevator. Naturally, on a day when she wanted to hurry, it was raining, a cold winter rain that bore the label 'made in Ontario'. And the car, sitting in the parking lot beside the building, refused to start.

What do you do with a car that won't start? Stacey knew a great deal more about cars now than she had three months ago, but was not about to be analytical. Either you loved it or you abused it! In her gloomy rain-ridden mind she was not about to spare a little love for an automobile. She banged the steering wheel three or four times, bruising the palm of her hand in the process, then applied half a dozen words she had heard when she was an 'Army brat'. The car was sufficiently impressed by it all, and started immediately. Her fingers tingled from the impact. She looked down, remembered, and blushed.

Harry had been in the bedroom when she came out of

the shower, wearing a nightgown that clung to her now, due to the steamy bathroom. 'That's what I forgot!' She held both palms up to her cheeks to hide the blush. 'My rings! I—I threw them at you!'

'And I caught them,' he chuckled. 'I played short stop for SMU in my college days. Now, where the devil did I put them?' He fished in the pockets of his robe, and came out triumphantly.

'You kept them? You carried them around with you?'

'A fellow never knows when he needs a wife,' he had said, pompously. 'Now, let me see.' He picked up her left hand and gently threaded her fingers through the two rings.

'Oh, but that's not—that's beautiful!' She held up her hand admiringly, watching the light sparkle from a delicate diamond-studded band next to the familiar wedding ring she had worn. 'It's not—'

'No, it isn't Grandmother's ring,' he said softly. 'I could see you were upset by that ring. It was too garish—too ornate. But I saw this one in Dallas one day, and it was just like you, slender and sparkling with life. I just had to have it. Do you approve?'

'Oh yes.' Her voice was as soft as a sigh running down the wind. His arms came around her, treasuring her. For just a moment she could almost think it was real. But the shadow of Lisette was too dark on her mind. She had to ask.

'Lisette,' she questioned. 'Did you love her very much?'

'Love her?' There was a stern strange look in his eyes as if he were seeing beyond them both, beyond the walls, beyond the years. 'Stacey,' he sighed, 'I've only ever loved one woman in all my life.'

And now, sitting in the car, the motor running, she was sorry she had asked. She shifted into gear, bucked and stuttered down to Fifth Street, drove under the shadow of the expressway, and found not a single parking space available on the campus.

Her bitterness bred defiance. She pulled up in front of the Administration building and parked in the spot marked 'Distinguished Visitors'. One of the campus police started in her direction, but she fled into the rain before he arrived. All of which brought her into Professor Calnan's class ten minutes late, soaking wet, and fully prepared to be the butt of all the 'guinea-pig' jokes. Which she was.

By lunchtime her anger had boiled over twice—once at a perfectly innocent Junior who had been trying to date her for weeks, the other at her History professor, who had a somewhat limited view about the participation of women in the world's scene. The boy backed off quickly enough when Stacey flashed her rings under his nose, and mentioned how big her *husband* was. The professor also retired from the field, under her barrage of feminist responses. It didn't help that the rest of the class cheered her on. They would have done anything to break up a Monday morning lecture.

Which brought her to lunch. She could hardly face the thought of food, so she went back to the car, settled back on one of the reclining seats, and promptly went to sleep, missing both her afternoon classes.

What woke her up was a sharp movement of the car. She sat up, startled, to find a tow-truck about to take her and her car away to the impound centre. And that was the last straw. She came out of the vehicle like an avenging angel, stormed at the policeman, then spared a little vitriol for the driver of the tow-truck. It had been a long time since the US Army had used mules for its artillery, but the mule-driving language still persisted, as any Army brat could testify.

'And I wasn't parked,' she finally threw at them both, her face red with rage. 'If you'd looked you could have seen that I was trying to repair my car! But you didn't look, did you? You didn't even know I was in there!' And with that atrocious lie on her conscience she climbed back in the Eagle, waited barely a moment for them to uncouple the cable, and drove off. The black rage settled a few blocks away, when she recognised that she was driving in the wrong direction, and was now in the middle of Oakwood Cemetery.

'Stop here!' she yelled at herself. The car swerved to the kurb, almost at the feet of a startled maintenance man. Stacey smiled sweetly at him, then started counting backwards from two hundred down.

And thus back to the Marsden building, driving sedately, wondering how she might explain it all to Harry.

It really didn't matter. Harry was in conference when she arrived, and she spent another half-hour reading old magazines in the waiting room. 'And just why am I worried?' she mumbled to herself. 'I'm not responsible to Harry. He's not my father or anything!'

'What's that?' asked Amie as she came through.

'Nothing,' mumbled Stacey. 'I was talking to myself, is all.'

'Well, he'll be another hour, at least,' Amie returned. 'He suggests that you go on up and have a nap. He'll come when he can.'

But even in the soft comfort of the waterbed Stacey was unable to sleep. By the time Harry *did* come she had managed to convince herself that the whole terrible day was entirely his fault. As a result, the greeting he received was just this side of glacial, and the trip out to the mansion was made in complete silence. When he parked in front of the house he took her arm as she tried to climb out, and she was unable to escape.

'I can see something's wrong,' he said, 'and we'd better get it settled before we go in. Was it because of last night?'

He pulled her over against him, burying her head in his chest. For a moment she beat on him with her clenched fists. 'It's all your fault,' she sobbed. 'Everything is all your fault!'

'Of course it is,' he soothed, stroking her hair. 'Everything is my fault. Tell me about your day.'

She did, between tears and hiccups. All the details, including the sneer on the professor's lips, and the policeman's threat to have her arrested and locked up. 'And he said I was a menace to society, and they would lock me up and throw away the key, and—'

'There, there,' he sighed, squeezing her shoulder. 'He won't do that—I won't let him. What else happened?' Stacey poured the rest of her day on to his broad shoulders and then sat up and dried her eyes.

'I'm all right,' she whispered to him, and knew she was. Nothing could touch her. He wouldn't let them!

'Sure you are.' He handed her his big handkerchief. 'Blow.'

She sniffed a couple of times, ran a hand through her hair to straighten out the mess, adjusted her blouse, and folded her hands primly in her lap.

'Should I have changed?' she asked in a very small voice.

'No,' he returned. 'I doubt if Lisette is up.'

'Did you tell her about me?'

'Well, I—' It was still light enough for her to see his face, as it flushed under the tan.

'You didn't, did you! I have to do that myself?'

'I'm afraid so,' he mumbled. 'I seemed to have lost my courage when the time was right. You don't mind?'

'I don't mind,' she sighed. 'It's just policemen and provosts and cynical professors that scare me.' And you, when you're angry, she wanted to add, but dared not. 'I'm ready.'

It was like coming home. Harry held the door for her, and it seemed as if the house reached out to welcome her. Everything was as it had been; perhaps a little shabbier, a little more dusty—but home. She saw it all now with new eyes—the dark mahoganies of the panelling, the slightly curved main stairs, the bric-à-brac scattered throughout the hall. Paintings. She had seen them all before, but never noticed them. The Marsden family ancestors? A small sigh of contentment welled up as she looped her hand through the crook of his arm and just stared. He patted her hand like some proud proprietor, and smiled that teasing half-smile that transformed his face.

And that's something else, she told herself. He's becoming more handsome all the time! It must be the weather, or—or what? Lisette? Just the thought was enough to send little spasms of monstrous jealousy coursing through her. Her smile vanished and she withdrew her hand. Harry was about to say something when the kitchen door, under the stairs, banged with a vengeance, and Millie Fallon came surging out into the hall.

'And that's the last straw!' Millie yelled at him, her angular face riven by anger. 'Up and down, up and down—you'd think I had a pogo stick, the way she wants and gives orders. Stood right here, she did, ordered her lunch in bed, then walked upstairs like some queen. There's nothing wrong with that girl, Harry, when you're not in the house! Well, not this time!'

She banged the heavy tray down on a side table and folded her arms belligerently across her bosom. And only then did she see Stacey, half hidden behind his frame. 'Oh, my Stacey! Lord, it's good to see you back home! It must have been terrible having to nurse your aunt for such a long time. Welcome. Frank will be so tickled that you're back. He always did have an eye for the good-looking girls.' She waded forward and embraced the younger woman, smothering her in aprons and love.

'Of course he does,' Stacey chuckled. 'That's why he married you!'

'When we get to the end of this meeting of the Mutual Admiration Society perhaps someone will tell me what's going on? I didn't hire you out to wait hand and foot on Lisette. What happened to the new girl?'

'Quit, that's what happened.' Millie stepped back

from Stacey and glared at him. 'I hired two of them, to
share the load. The first one quit at noontime, and the
second just walked out a few minutes ago. It seems that
our fair lady said some unpleasant things in very foul
language, then threw a pitcher of water all over her.'

'But she's sick, Millie.' Stacey did her best to pour a
little oil on the troubled waters, but it was plain that the
housekeeper was in no mood to be passified.

'Yeah, sick,' she snorted. 'She couldn't hardly eat any
dinner last night when Mr Harry was here. And then as
soon as he's out of the house she must have a double
snack, and a midnight supper, as well as half a dozen
drinks. And now look at this! She won't be down for
dinner tonight, she tells me, but will I please send
up—well, take a look.'

The tray was crowded. Harry snorted, and Stacey
giggled. A coffee pot and cup, a Bloody Mary in a curved
wine glass, two hefty roast beef sandwiches, and a dozen
assorted cookies.

'It looks as if she has consumption instead of TB,'
Stacey commented.

'That's a lousy pun,' he snapped. 'I'm sure there's
some reasonable explanation.'

'I'm sure there is too,' grated Millie. 'Why don't you
take this tray up and ask her?'

'All right, all right.' Stacey stepped between them.
'Retire to a neutral corner, both of you. I'll take it up.
Put my jacket away, Millie?'

'Oh, love,' the housekeeper sighed, 'I didn't mean to
get you into the puddle, and on your first night home,
too.'

'Don't be a ninny,' Stacey returned. 'That's my job,
isn't it? Who's the mistress of this house?'

'Well—why, of course you are. Here, let me take that.
Harry, look at this coat! Aren't you ashamed of yourself,
having your wife run around in rags and tatters? And
those blue jeans—lordy, I've seen prisoners working on
the road gangs in better clothes than that!'

'Don't look at me,' Harry laughed. 'I don't have a thing to say about what she wears—or much else around here, apparently. But come right back, wife. We'll have our dinner in the—'

'In the kitchen, Millie,' Stacey interrupted. 'There's no need to carry all those dishes to the dining room when there's only the family. You lay the table, set the food on the stove, then you and Frank go take a night off. I'll take care of everything else.'

'Why, indeed you will,' the housekeeper chuckled. 'How you've changed! You were only a slip of a girl when you first came, and now look at how you've grown!'

Stacey was juggling the tray when the unexpected compliment caught up with her. She looked around quickly to surprise a strange look on Harry's face, a look she could not identify. But it quickly fled, to be replaced by one of his 'I am King of the Hill' expressions. She winked at Millie anyway, and started up the stairs.

The tray was heavy, one of the old silver services his grandmother had treasured but had never taken out of the china closet. And that's another problem, Stacey noted. All of a sudden there's a panoply of glory around the place. More of Harry's doings? Are we celebrating the greening of Lisette Langloise? 'Well, I hope it chokes her,' she muttered, then stopped in midstride to berate herself. 'That's the way children talk,' she lectured. 'If you expect Harry to think you've grown up you have to prove it!' And there's no argument there, she assured herself bitterly. Nevertheless, she rested the tray for a moment on a chair in the hall, ran a quick hand through her hair, brushed down her blouse, and checked all the buttons. Then she plastered a smile on her face, turned the door knob, and carried the tray into the bedroom.

It was the same room that Grandmother Marsden had used for so long, the room in which she had had her first and last look at the indomitable old woman. There had been a massive rearrangement. All the drapes and heavy furniture were gone, replaced by light modern things, flower-sprayed wallpaper, concealed lighting, and a Hollywood type queen-sized bed.

And the queen bee was sitting beside the bed, prepared to sting!

'Oh, good heavens, another ragbag! Don't they have anyone in that kitchen who knows how to dress?' The voice might once have been a lovely soprano, but now it cracked and was hoarse. It emanated from a tiny body, hardly more than five feet tall, slender as a willow, with a dark thin face surrounded by a halo of raven hair. The woman wore the gamine look of a Parisienne, outfitted in harem pyjamas with a light negligee thrown over the whole.

Stacey set the tray down on the table in front of the dormer window and turned around. 'Miss Langloise? I'm—'

'Mrs Burnet,' the other woman snapped. 'Mrs Burnet. Call me ma'am. Doesn't anybody ever teach you girls anything? Don't you own a dress?'

Stacey looked down at her own extended hand and laughed. Six months ago she would have been in tears, terrified out of her mind. But now it was just funny.

'Mrs Burnet? OK. That makes it easier, I suppose.' She looked down at her ragged jeans. 'Perhaps I should have changed.' She smiled, remembering the conversation downstairs. 'But then again, I only dress to please Harry, you know, and he was perfectly content with these. The coffee is very warm. Do you want me to pour you a cup? I can only stay a minute, but perhaps that's enough time for us to get acquainted.'

'Don't count on it,' Lisette snapped. 'You don't seem any better than the other two. What happened to them?'

'Oh, they both quit their jobs,' Stacey said quietly. 'Of course I'll have Harry find them something else to do. Nobody ever loses their job in Marsden Enterprises.'

'Whatever in the world are you talking about?' There was more than puzzlement on Lisette's face, there was the beginning of anger. Her rather ordinary face began to glow from the inside, adding a look of sensuous beauty. There! That's what attracted Harry, she told herself. She's beautiful when she's angry, and I expect that's most of the time. I've only ever loved one woman in all my life—isn't that what Harry said? And this must be the one.

'All right, who are you?' Lisette's snarl snapped Stacey back to attention.

'Me? My name is Marsden,' she lied. It was becoming easier, much easier. 'Stacey Marsden. I thought you knew.'

'No, I don't know.' Stacey could actually see the wheels revolving in the older woman's brain, as she ran through the geneology of the family. 'Stacey? Stacey Marsden? I don't remember anyone by that name in the family, and I knew them all. What the hell is this? Some sort of a con game?'

'I don't think so.' Stacey busied herself around the bed, picking up discarded magazines, emptying an overflowing ashtray into the wastebasket, keeping her head down. 'Perhaps you'd recognise me better by my formal name? I'm Mrs Harry Marsden.'

The screech that followed shook the heavy windows in their ancient casings. 'You're a damn liar!' the other woman shouted. She staggered to her feet, glaring enough to kill. 'Nobody does that to me—nobody!'

'Then I guess I don't know what your problem is,' Stacey answered quietly. 'Harry and I were married just before his grandmother died. It's been some time. We had been hoping that by this time I would be—well—of course, there's no way to guarantee that!' Stop padding your part, her conscience nagged at her. If you get yourself tangled up in the 'patter of little feet' routine, there's no telling where it all will end! Keep to the straight and narrow. Uncle Henry had said that once—if you have to lie, keep it simple. And who would know better than Uncle Henry? 'Are you not really feeling well, Mrs Burnet?'

'No, I'm not feeling well. Help me get back to bed. I've—I must be having a reaction to the medicine.' Sure you are, Stacey chuckled to herself. But you're not taking any! She moved, nevertheless, and helped the other woman under the covers. As she looked down at the troubled little face she felt just a touch of sympathy, but she drew herself up fiercely. It's Harry she wants, she told herself grimly. *My* Harry. Anything goes. All's fair in love and whatever! She patted down the blankets, checked to make sure that the push-bell was near to hand, and started for the door. Behind her in the bed she could hear a mumbling, rising in volume but still incomprehensible. Without looking back, Stacey lengthened her stride and hurried out of the room.

Just in time, apparently. Something crashed against the other side of the door she had just closed behind her. She leaned against it, half in tears, half in laughter, clutching at her stomach to still the aching created by giggles. 'The medicine's too strong for you, baby, isn't it?' she commented, and made her way around to the other wing, where her own little suite—and Harry's—waited.

It was a strange evening that followed. Stacey shared a homey dinner with Harry, serving his plate directly from the stove, wishing she could produce as nice a meal as Millie had left. After dinner they stacked the dishes in the dishwasher, and prepared a light tray for Lisette—a vegetable salad, a paper-thin slice of steak, a spoonful of mashed potatoes garlanded with a cherry at its peak, and a pot of tea.

'That looks just what an invalid ought to eat,' Harry commented, clapping her on the shoulder. She knew he was being gentle, but her shoulder almost collapsed.

'Then why don't you take it up?' She turned her head away quickly to hide the smile, but it felt as if he were boring holes in the back of her neck, understanding her every ploy before it was executed.

'Don't be sarcastic, Kitten, it doesn't become you. She *is* an invalid, you know.'

'I know she is. And don't call me Kitten—I hate that. That's *her* name.' Stacey was applying her father's axiom: the best defence is a good offence. But Harry was insufferably unconquered. Damn the man!

'Why not both of us together?' he suggested. 'Togetherness? Love and closeness, all that?'

'Why not?' she muttered. Indeed, why not. It ought to be worth the price of admission. She picked up the tray, a light plastic one she had resurrected from under the kitchen counter, and started for the stairs. Harry relieved her of the weight, using one hand, and slipped the other around her waist as they went up the stairs, side by side. His touch startled her, but there was something more than that. Her eye was on the tray as they climbed, and at the very second his hand closed on her waist, the tray in his other hand jumped and almost spilled the teapot off on to the rug. So there, she told herself! He's not all that impervious after all!

They went into the room the same way, he with his arm tightened around her slenderness, she handling the doorknob as if it might explode in her face.

It was an entirely different woman that she saw. Still reclining in bed, with two pillows at her back, Lisette Burnet had changed into a very demure granny gown, high-buttoned and flower-decorated. Her hair sparkled from brushing, her face was carefully and smoothly made up, and she had become the perfect picture of an enticing invalid.

'Harry,' she cooed, 'how nice of you to go to all this trouble! And your little wife, too. I was so surprised when I met her this evening—she seems like such a lovable child. And you both brought my dinner. I don't have much of an appetite, of course.'

Harry busied himself setting up the tray on her knees,

all solicitude and charm. Stacey gritted her teeth and went over to draw the curtains. By the time she returned they were deep in conversation, the 'do you remember when' type, that filled the air with names and times and places, all strange to Stacey. Once Harry made an attempt to draw her into it, but Lisette quickly manoeuvred around the subject to exclude her again.

Oh well, she told herself, what would you expect? They grew up together. But what an act that is! All love and delight. To give her credit, in the soft light of the lamps the older woman did not look her age. The lighting and her make-up had done wonders. *Now, Stacey*, her conscience tickled, she's ill—you can see the marks of it on her face. Her hair is fading from it. She deserves the comfort. And if I were the Christian I was raised to be, I'd be helping, instead of standing here like a blithering idiot, berating her.

In a blush of guilt Stacey looked around for something to do. They were too engrossed now to remember she was present. The closet doors stood open, and clothes were strewn around in heaps. She didn't just accidentally find that demure little nightgown, Stacey told herself, as her fingers busied at smoothing and sorting and re-hanging. And then there was the silver tray to be squared away. Empty, she noted. All the sandwiches and cookies gone, the pot drained—and now she's struggling with the dinner!

'It's just too much for me,' Lisette sighed. 'I have so little appetite these days, Harry.'

'Of course,' he returned heartily. 'That's to be expected. But you have to keep your strength up. These mashed potatoes are a delight. She puts a little cheese in them, and a touch of some herb that I don't remember. Open up.'

My God, he's going to hand-feed her, Stacey muttered to herself. What a glorious act this is! But why does it bother me, that's the question. Why? It wouldn't have taken her more than a minute or two to wrestle with the problem and find an answer. But she also knew it was an answer she didn't want to hear, so she pushed it away.

The pair of them were at it again, bent close to each other in the lamplight. Occasionally Harry would make some soft comment, underlined by his deep bass chuckle. And Lisette would counterpoint with her high shrill soprano. The only interruptions came when Lisette stopped to light another one of her interminable cigarettes. One for my side, Stacey mused; Harry really hates to see women smoking. She hugged that tiny bit of warmth to her as the recollections dragged on. But eventually it all began to get under her skin. The game had sounded fine the first time around, but now its ragged edges were beginning to show. After all, it had been Lisette who had gone away. I wish I knew more about that, Stacey thought, but I've had about as much of this as I can stand for one night.

She tapped Harry on the shoulder. He turned around, looking as if he were startled to see her, as if he had forgotten her existence. 'It's been a long day,' she said quietly, 'and I still have a load of studies to work through. If you two will excuse me, I'll take this tray down to the kitchen and clean up.'

'Studies?' Lisette looked up at her with an eager smile.

'Yes,' Harry responded. 'Stacey is enrolled at Baylor. We thought she ought to finish up, but Grandmother wouldn't hear of delaying the wedding. She wanted so much to see it accomplished.' He checked his wrist-watch. 'And I guess it's late enough for both of us to bustle off. Get your beauty sleep, Lisette. I'm not going in to work tomorrow, so we'll have plenty of time to talk.'

'You could stay, Harry,' the woman invited. 'I'm sure your bride won't be able to do much studyings with you around.'

'Yes, well—perhaps,' he laughed. 'But to tell the

truth, I—er—help her out. After all, we've only been married a few months, Lisette. You get your rest.'

'If you insist, Harry.' The words were buttery. Nothing that Harry wants can be wrong! Stacey stumbled for the tray, only to have it taken from her immediately. But before she could sort out the dishes to be carried down, he swept her up in his arms, brooded over her for a moment, then leaned down to seal her lips with his. Whatever it had been meant to be—deception, greeting, whatever—it turned itself into a fiery volcano of passion that left her hanging in his arms, gasping. And over his should she could see a very thoroughly dissatisfied Lisette, glaring at them both.

'Excuse us,' Harry called over his shoulder as he helped Stacey to the door with one hand, and balanced the silver tray in the other. 'We'll see you in the morning, my dear.'

My dear? After withering me with that—that kiss, he calls *her* my dear? Why, I'll—Whatever it was she would, Harry squeezed it all out of her with a massive hug that left fingerprints on her ribcage, and hurried her out of the room and down the hall. She forced him to a stubborn stop at the head of the stairs.

'We're off stage now,' she snapped at him. 'Let me go, you monstrous—'

Harry put one finger over her lips. 'She has remarkably good hearing,' he whispered in her ear. 'Was there something wrong with that kiss?'

'You know darned well there wasn't, you—you lecher,' she snapped. 'It was that whole ball of wax in there. Gee, do you remember? What is it she's trying to do—lure you back into your cage, or something?'

'I do believe you're jealous.' He chuckled softly, as if the idea were very pleasant to him.

'Jealous be darned,' she snarled. 'Oh, my dear Harry!' She did her best to mimic Lisette's trill. 'And after that you display your gorilla act. What the devil do you think I am, made of cast steel or something?'

'Did I hurt you?' He was all solicitude, but somehow or another she got the impression that it was all a put-on.

'No, you didn't hurt me,' she raged. 'You only managed to crack two or three ribs, I think.'

'Good Lord, did I?'

'Yes, you did!' It was hard not to giggle, even though her side was truly bruised. There was such a twinkle in his eyes, and his voice dripped honey all over the conversation. He set the tray down on the rug and pulled her around to face him.

'Honest Injun?' he asked solemnly.

Stacey nodded her head. Before she could react further Harry swept her off her feet and went stalking down the corridor to the other wing, where their suite was arranged. The door was open. He closed it behind them with a hard click of his heel, fingered the overhead lights on, and carried her over to the fourposter.

'Now what in the world are you doing!'

'Checking up,' he said briefly. 'It doesn't pay to have an injured member in the cast. Especially when it's the star of the show.' He dropped her unceremoniously on top of the bed and watched while she bounced and vibrated.

'That's a rotten thing to do,' she snapped at him. 'I might have a punctured lung or something. Leave me alone!'

'Maybe,' he mused. He put one hand flat on her chest, just below her throat, and held her in place while the other hand tugged the tails of her blouse free from her jeans and began to unsnap the line of buttons that held it closed.

'What are you *doing*?'

'I'm looking for bruises,' he replied mildly, as his hands continued on their errand. 'No time for a bra today, love?'

'Mind your own business,' she retorted stiffly. She was

doing her best to discipline a recalcitrant body, and not having an great deal of luck at it. Every spot his fingers touched seemed to catch on fire, the whole feeling gathering together quickly into a massive fire-storm that was beyond her control. But control she must! Don't think about it, her conscience dictated. Count. Count to a thousand! She started off, but lost her place somewhere beyond eleven, when one of his hands turned her on her side, cruising just over the tip of her breast to do so.

'Yes, I *did* do something,' he commented, tracing a finger around the sore area. 'That's terrible. I just don't seem to know my own strength.'

'You can say that again,' Stacey gritted through clenched teeth. 'Now will you let me be?'

'An ice pack,' he continued, as if she had said nothing. 'That's what we need.'

'I don't need an ice park,' she screeched at him. 'What I need is a great deal of privacy!'

'Yes, well, that's something that's hard to come by,' he chuckled as he gently pulled her blouse back together and re-buttoned it. 'Try a cold shower.'

'I don't need a cold shower for my bruises,' she stormed at him.

'Not for your bruises, but you do need a cold shower.' His finger tilted her chin up so she was forced to look into his eyes. 'You're shaking like a bowl of jelly. Just look at you!'

She jerked away from him. 'Please get out of here and leave me alone!' she snapped.

'Of course,' he said softly, dropped the teasing tone that had aggravated her so much. He walked over to the door, then came back. 'I don't know how you feel about Lisette, but you were surely a shock to *her*.'

'I—I did all right? I'm not much of an actress.'

'You did more than all right,' chuckled Harry. 'You were superior. I'm afraid, in all the confusion, I haven't told you often enough how well you play your part,

Stacey. You fit in perfectly. It means a lot to me.' He sat down at the foot of the bed, and strangely enough, it didn't seem to bother her.

'You and Lisette—you were close?'

'When we were kids, yes. After she got to high school it was a different story. But yes, we were close. She was important to me—still is, I guess.'

'Still important to you? So important that you had to hire a bride for protection?' It was hard for her to keep the bitter edge off the words.

'Important, yes. But marriage never entered my thoughts. She and I have often agreed to differ about that subject. No, what I meant was that Grandmother left me a charge in regard to Lisette, and I want to do everything I can to make it all come out right for her. Up to a point, that is. And that's where you come in. You know, Stacey, you *have* changed a great deal in these past few months. Amie told me about your ambitions. It's good to see you take control of your own life. And before you ask, no, I don't think of you as some child cluttering up the landscape. Does that make you feel better?'

'Yes!' She managed a smile. 'And you didn't really break my ribs—I was just angry.'

'I know. But you'd better get some rest, and do that studying of yours.'

'I made that up,' she said shyly. 'It's English tomorrow—Emerson and the New England poets. I read all that years ago. And Mr Herndon snapped the whip over my head about it just a little time ago. After Mr Herndon, this college material is a snap.'

Harry smiled at her enthusiasm. 'Mr Herndon?'

'My tutor. I—somebody hired him to tutor me, so I could qualify for my High School Equivalency exam. He's a nice man.'

'Oh, I know that,' he chuckled. 'He was the Assistant Superintendent of schools in Waco before he retired. What other little gimmicks are you working on?'

'Nothing,' she half whispered. 'I just want to get my degree, that's all.'

'Come to think of it,' he mused, as he got ot his feet, 'I made a small mistake there. Amie didn't tell me about your ambitions, she told me about your immediate goals. Which means there's something more behind all this sudden spurt of work, isn't there? Care to tell me about it?'

'No, I don't think I do,' she said primly. 'I mean, there's nothing else—and if there were, perhaps I wouldn't care to tell you about it. I'm entitled to my own secrets.'

'Methinks the lady doth protest too much.' Harry touched one finger lightly on the tip of her nose. 'Get on with it,' he concluded. 'The world opens up to the educated. And whatever your ambition, I wish you well of it.'

Me too, thought Stacey, as he strolled through the door. Me too. And I can't possibly tell you. How do you go about stating your final objective to the one who is it—your final objective, that is?

It's a strange, upsetting household, she mused. But no matter how many troubles there are, I can't help smiling. The world seems—better, over here. And I don't know why. Don't I? She was singing an advertising jingle as she picked up her night things and went into the bathroom. Cold shower, indeed! She giggled at the idea, and after a long warm dousing, gave it a try. The water came out as cold as a Witches' Sabbath, and she was unable to find the faucet handle to turn it down. Shrieking and laughing at the same time, she stumbled out of the shower cubicle into a huge warm towel held by huge warm arms.

'You're red all over,' Harry commented solemnly as he rubbed her briskly.

'A real gentleman would never have looked,' she snapped at him. But her heart wasn't in the squabble. It's no use fighting against him: that was the one con-

clusion that the cold shower had brought her to. Let
be what will be—that was another saying of her
father's. And now Harry bundled her into the towel as
if it were a sarong, then pulled another towel from the
warming rail and swathed her hair in it.

'What's this all about?' she asked, warm again under
the massage that continued through the towels.

'I went downstairs,' he said, 'and then I remembered
something important I'd forgotten to tell you about. As I
came back up I noticed that our house guest was out and
wandering.'

'So you came immediately into my bathroom?'

'Our bathroom,' he corrected. 'Now come on—show
time!'

He pulled her out into the bedroom, teasing and
tickling as they went. They fell in a heap on the foot of
the bed. Harry was on the bottom, still massaging her
hair. Stacey, on top, wiggled to get free, not really
meaning it. In her exertions the knot on her towel
slipped, and it fell to her waist, leaving her almost nude,
sitting in his lap and giggling happily. He took one more
swipe at her hair and flicked that towel away on to the
floor. His hands came down hungrily on her bare
shoulders, manipulating her against his soaked shirt.
And at that moment the door opened, and Lisette came
in.

They both stopped their game and stared at her.
Lisette's eyes inspected them carefully, swung to the
mussed bed, and returned. 'Well, I *am* sorry,' she
drawled. 'I was exploring the house for old times' sake,
and I didn't realise that you—'

'Lisette,' said Harry reproachfully, moving one hand
to restore Stacey's towel, 'surely you can see we're—
occupied at the moment. Would you excuse us, please?'

The older woman was definitely not pleased at the
tableau. To emphasise the point, one of his hands came
around under the curve of Stacey's breast, and hovered
there. She did her best to contain her reflex action, but it

was a hard struggle. Lisette stared at them both for another moment, then turned slowly and went out, slamming the door behind her.

'Okay, you can breathe now,' he chuckled.

'What?'

'You're turning blue, love. Start breathing, or I'll have to apply the kiss of life. Is that what you want?'

'Huh? Oh no—certainly not! Let me down, please, and—' again that telltale squeak of alarm—'I mean *with* the towel too! I'm not running a free peepshow!' She stomped over to the other side of the bed and perched there. 'And that's another thing,' she stated flatly.

'What? Locks on the doors? No peeking until Sundays?'

'No, silly. That waterbed has got to go!'

'What in the world brought that into the conversation?'

'Never you mind. Just mark it down in your little book. The waterbed has got to go! You hear?'

'I imagine that everybody in McClennan County can hear. Okay, the waterbed has got to go. Seasick, were you?'

'No. You knew she'd come up here to my—to our bedroom, didn't you!'

'Yes.'

'Rat! What was it that you wanted to tell me?'

'Oh, I almost forgot again. Seeing little Miss Langloise pussyfooting down the hall knocked it out of my mind.'

'Mrs—little Mrs Burnet,' corrected Stacey. 'She gave me what-for when I used the wrong title.'

'Ah. And what did you tell her?'

'I told her that I was big Mrs Harry Marsden. She didn't seem to like that. What was the other thing?'

'The other thing? Oh Lord, yes—the other thing.' Harry picked himself up from the bed and moved gingerly over to the rickety chair. 'As you must know,' he continued, 'I hired a firm of international private detectives to run—Mrs Burnet to ground. And while I was at it I had them keep an eye open for your Uncle Henry.'

'Henry Delano?'

'The very man.'

'And?'

'And I met him in Paris too. We had a long talk. He's not as mean a man as he used to be—having a packet of money seems to have lessened his animosity. Did you know that he took you for almost seven hundred thousand dollars? He's invested it comfortably in French government securities, and is living with a woman near the Paris Opera House.'

'What should I say? That's nice? Or something like that? Was George there?' She sounded calm, she thought. Good! How sophisticated did you have to be?

'No, evidently he dumped George, who's still somewhere in Texas, I'm told. But the old man was prepared to make some amends, providing you don't try to get him extradited to stand trial.'

'I don't care what becomes of him,' Stacey said quietly, 'just so long as he stays far away. That's all I want. Aunt Ellen—she hasn't said a great deal, but I suspect she would like to be free of him.'

'Yes, I thought so myself. So I took it upon myself, acting as your husband, to assure him that if he co-operated, nothing further would happen.'

'If he co-operated in what?'

'Well, he gave me a few papers that I brought back—affidavits, birth certificates, marriage licences—'

'Whoa—say that again! Marriage licences—plural?'

'That's right. Would you believe it, your Uncle Henry married your aunt without getting a divorce from his first wife. I've got it all in writing, at the office.'

'And that means?' asked Stacey.

'And that means that if she wants it, your aunt can have her marriage annulled. In fact, I've got a lawyer friend who could take it in hand and get it over with before she finishes her last operation. How about that?'

'Oh, you wonderful man!' She jumped up from the bed and threw herself at him, losing the towel in the process. His arms came around her again. 'You wonderful man!' she repeated.

'Yes, aren't I?' he said in that wondering voice. He looked down her long lush nude frame, and moistened his lips desperately. 'Lord, I've got to get out of here!' he groaned, and ran for the door.

CHAPTER NINE

THAT first week of living at Rosedale with Lisette was like taking up housekeeping on a roller-coaster. Stacey was hardly back from school for more than half an hour on Wednesday before she discovered that her guest had given up being an invalid and was downstairs, dressed in slacks and see-through blouse, giving orders which Millie was decidedly refusing to take.

'I take orders only from Mrs Marsden,' Stacey heard as she came down, having showered and changed. 'She's the mistress of the house, until I hear different from the mister.'

'We'll see about that—oh, hello Stacey.' The voice was shrill. Lisette had a half-filled glass of something in her hand, twirling it nervously so that the ice cube rang against the sides. Stacey checked the clock. Four-thirty, time for at least one of the chores she had set her mind on.

'Hello,' she offered quietly, then turned to the housekeeper. 'You got my note about the upstairs hall? And a new girl?'

'Yes,' Millie returned, 'I did manage to get a local girl, but she wants to live in. A hard worker, with plenty of references.'

'Live in? Sounds like a good idea. But you must warn her that it may only be temporary. These chocolate chip cookies are delicious, Millie. Well, I've intended to dust that bric-à-brac cabinet of Grandmother's ever since I first saw it, and today's the day. Care to give me a hand, Lisette?'

'Me? What a laugh! No, you go right ahead and get it all cleaned up for me.' There was a taunting laugh behind the words as she slurped at the glass. 'It won't be long before it's all mine, all this.'

'Well, you're half right anyway,' Stacey commented grimly. 'Where are those dust-cloths, Millie?'

That had been only the first week. By Friday night of the third week Stacey was totally discouraged. 'I don't think I can last out the whole three months,' she told Harry that night in the privacy of their room. 'She picks at everything I do, but won't offer a hand to help at all. And you noticed at dinner tonight? Every chance she gets, I'm a child. I just hope for your sake, Harry, that I can hold my temper.'

He shifted his weight in the big chair. That's *one* thing I've accomplished, she told herself—scouring the house to replace the dainty furniture with something substantial for him! 'Don't hold back on my account,' he said from behind his newspaper.

Funny I hadn't noticed that before, she told herself. Every night he hides behind his paper. I never get to see his face at all. And he pays my complaints about as much attention as they're worth—which is nothing! What is this? Some kind of message he's sending me? Don't tread on my Lisette?

She piled her knitting back into its bag and moved over to the footstool beside his chair, ready to fire a salvo in the war—well, at least the skirmish—for his attention.

'Did you know she spent the entire afternoon today in your study, making telephone calls? The bill this month will be out of this world.'

'Uhuh.' The paper did not come down, but it did rattle a bit as he changed pages.

'And she keeps asking me about the Delanos. Did you tell her about Uncle Henry?'

'Uhuh.'

'Does that mean that you did?'

'Uhuh.'

'She was terribly angry when Frank told her she couldn't ride the one Arab mare that's still here. He told her the horse wasn't well, and he was putting a hot poultice on her foreleg. But Lisette wouldn't take that for an excuse. She said she was going to ride the mare anyway.'

'Uhuh.'

'But I don't think the animal will ever recover. Very few do, after a crocodile bite, you know.'

Harry lowered his paper with a great sigh and folded it carefully into its proper sections. 'Why are you looking for a fight tonight?' he asked mildly. 'The way you keep nagging at me I might as well be married.'

Stacey's face turned a brilliant red. The idea had tremendous appeal, even though that wasn't what she had in mind when the discussion started. 'You weren't listening to a thing I said,' she snapped. 'I'm certainly learning a great deal around here. Everything *not to do* when I really get married!'

'I heard every word,' he sighed. 'Every word. Lisette is running up the telephone bill. Yes, she was present the first time I met your Uncle Henry, but that's all she knows about it. And you don't have to worry about the mare. Frank is taking her over this afternoon.

'Over where?'

'Over to Rancho Miraflores, of course. Where all the others have gone. Don't you keep in touch with your own ranch?'

'I—I've been busy—you know that! Why to—what's going on?'

'I explained it all once before,' he said quietly. 'Rosedale is all Lisette has left in the world. That bum she married left her nothing. As soon as the three-month period is up, she'll want to sell Rosedale, and I can't blame her.'

'You mean you'd give all this up? You never explained any such a thing to me, Harry Marsden. That's one of the problems around here. You never explain anything to me—not anything. Tell me about the Arabs!'

'Well, I didn't want to catch them up in all the

confusion of changing home pastures in the middle of May, so I've had them all shipped over to your ranch. Westland Cattle informed me that the new barn and paddocks were ready.'

'Without even consulting me?'

'You did give me your general power of attorney,' he reminded her. 'You want me to tear it up?'

'I—no. Dear Lord, no! I'm not *that* independent-minded.' Stacey edged her footstool an inch or two closer, and put her folded arms on his knees. 'Harry?' she asked tentatively. He smiled.

'Harry? What do you really do for a living? *Really*, I mean. How come your offices are in the choice spot at the top of the building, with a penthouse, no less?'

'Mostly because I own the building, Stacey. And a couple of other properties.'

'Oh, is *that* it! Of course, I should have guessed— Marsden Management. You manage real estate!'

'I guess you could say that,' he chuckled. 'Satisfied?'

'I—I guess so.' For the moment, you mean, her conscience dug at her. There are a million things more I'd like to know, but haven't the courage to ask. Now if I were a real wife I wouldn't stop until I knew everything about him. Look at me. I know what he likes for breakfast, what size all his clothes are, which silly gossip makes him angry, how his left eyebrow cocks up just the slightest when he's really puzzled. I know everything about him except where he's at. Isn't that silly? I'll never know him better until we share a—but that was asking too much. She pushed away from him and went back to her knitting. He watched her flying fingers, then added, 'And by the way, there aren't any crocodiles in the Western Hemisphere, only alligators.' And with that he dodged behind his paper again.

Stacey was still making her regular trips to Houston. Jim Morgan brought the helicopter up to the house. She was sure this time—he was wearing a T-shirt with his name scribbled on the chest.

Aunt Ellen was as chipper as one could ask. 'I'm ready for the second transplant,' she gurgled. 'Would you believe it, me looking forward to an operation? They're going to take this little piece of skin from the inside of my arm and replace that little section there—' She gestured awkwardly to the tiny section of her cheek still marked by the raspberry birthmark—'and then maybe that will be that. Stacey, I've met some of the nicest people you ever could see. There's a man who—but of course, that's out of the question.'

'Isn't there a phrase about striking while the iron's hot?' Stacey laughed as she told her aunt all about Henry Delano. When she had finished she noted a glisten in the older woman's eyes. 'It doesn't please you?'

'It pleases me very much,' her aunt sighed. 'I thought there might never be a way to be free of him, but then I had no reason to want to be free. I had no other plans, but—does this all sound confusing?'

'Not at all, love. Shall I tell Harry to go ahead full speed?'

'Yes, please, Stacey. My, how much that man has done for us! Your father would have been very pleased with your selection of a husband. You must treasure him, girl.'

That phrase stuck in Stacey's mind all the way back to Waco, flying in the darkness under IFR—Instrument Flight Regulations—in order to complete her licence requirements.

'Bang on the nose,' Jim told her as she flashed on the landing lights and made an approach to the pasture behind the house. 'Suppose I make an appointment for you for next month?'

'Do you really think I'm ready, Jim?'

'John,' he corrected. 'I had to borrow Jim's shirt this morning. Our laundry problem seems to be growing, now that you're not around any more. Yes, you're more than ready. Why don't you get in some solo time? There are three choppers and four fixed wings down at the airport. Just go down there and introduce yourself.'

It was the start of a new adventure. On Tuesday, when she had only one early class and one late one, and on Thursday, when she had no classes at all, she fell into a pattern. She took her Eagle to school with her, and in between classes squeezed in a few hours of flight time. There had not been a bit of trouble at the airport, where a separate hangar with the Marsden Management logo over the office door stood at an isolated end of the field. At least there was no trouble after the first few minutes, when a dubious flight manager had been about to turn down her request.

Stacey, with more courage than she had shown in the past five years, ran a bluff on him. She picked up his telephone and dialled Amie Moreland's number. Amie herself answered. Stacey passed the telephone, without a word, to the flight manager.

'There's this woman down here who says she's Mrs Marsden,' he started to say, then listened for a time. 'Yeah—about five foot ten, blonde hair, young, stacked like a brick—oh, excuse me, Mrs Moreland. And I can what? Anything? It'll cost a bundle in fuel—oh, on the boss's account? And if there's a scheduling problem? First priority? Well, okay, but I'd feel better if I had it in writing. No! No, ma'am, I didn't mean I couldn't take your word—yes, ma'am.' He put the handset down very carefully. 'She hung up on me,' he sighed. 'Lord, I hate to work for a woman. Oh—I don't mean nothing by that, Mrs Marsden. You can have anything you want—two of anything. The whole shootin' match, if you want.'

Stacey had used the new authority to its fullest, not only to get in her helicopter flight time, but also to take the minimum instruction in fixed wing flight. It was her release valve, that bled off all her bad temper, and allowed her to go back to Rosedale at the end of each day with her chin up.

March came in like a lion, bringing spring with it. Winter's cold grip was pried loose from the midlands, and the world took on a happier look. Even the animals at the Central Texas Zoo, adjacent to the airfield, took on a new life. And then March went out like a lion, and only Lisette had not responded to the change of season.

Instead of improving, she was looking more and more haggard. And more shrewish. Several times she commanded Frank to drive her, and made stops in Waco and Temple. 'I dunno what she's doin',' Frank reported. 'Them's some strange places she goes to. Got a lot of friends, she says, but I ain't seen any of them.'

Lisette always seemed to have a glass in her hand, morning, noon and night. And never a kind word for anyone except Harry. She came back late on the first of April, and was unusually excited at dinner.

'It won't be long, Harry,' she announced. 'Another month. Have you thought it over?'

'You mean your proposition about Rosedale?'

'Yes. What else is there to talk about?'

'Not now, Lisette. Stacey isn't interested. Find something that we can all talk about.'

'With that child, Harry? What in the world were you thinking of!'

'I've had it with that *child* business,' Stacey stormed at her. 'I'm not a child!' But the look in Lisette's gleaming eyes was enough to tell her that she had blown it all—had demonstrated that she *was* just a child.

'All you need to do is prove it,' the older woman answered coldly. 'Just how old are you, child?'

'I—none of your darn business,' Stacey snapped back. She sat rigidly upright at the table, immersed in her misery, and felt the drops cascading down into her soup. She fumbled for her napkin.

'There's another interesting thing,' Lisette continued. 'I heard tell you were engaged to someone else—a really torrid relationship—before Harry snapped you up. His name was—well, it just slips my mind at the moment.' She patted her lips daintily with her napkin, and turned her guns on Harry.

'You know a funny thing,' she gurgled, 'nobody seems to be able to find just where it was that you got married. Isn't that a surprise?'

'Don't you think you've had enough target practice for one night?' Harry grumbled at her. 'So Stacey is a lot younger than you are—so what? It's a problem she'll grow out of gradually.'

'Don't tell me that, Harry Marsden,' the woman seethed. 'I know you too well, man and boy. If that isn't guilt, I don't know what is!'

'Then you don't know a thing,' Harry returned. The lines on his face had reappeared, the craggy stern lines that Stacey had come to understand. Lines of strength. Lines of anger. He pushed his chair back from the table, came around, and tugged Stacey up. 'I would think that even a sophisticate like you could read the cards better,' he snapped. 'Stacey and I have been married for almost six months now, and women in her condition tend to get a little weepy and despondent now and then!'

'Damn you! Damn you both!' Lisette jumped to her feet, upsetting her heavy chair and sending it toppling into the corner. 'You rotten—' And then in a high-pitched shriek, 'You deserve each other, you pair of—'

The rest of the conversation was lost as she slammed the dining room door behind her. Mrs Fallon opened it, and stuck her head around the jam. 'She didn't like the soup?' she asked whimsically. It was just the right note. Stacey leaned against Harry, caught up in comfort, and cried until her eyes could shed no more. He wiped her eyes, furnished a handkerchief for her nose, then they both resumed their seats and went on with the meal as if nothing had happened.

But something had crystallised. From that day on Lisette did her best to avoid Stacey, remaining in bed until the younger girl had gone off to school, eating alone from a tray in her room, spending hours locked up with the telephone.

Something else occurred, too. Harry was worried about something. He spent a great many hours walking in the empty paddocks, alone by choice. Stacey would have loved to join him, but he refused her company. So she spent an equal amount of time at her bedroom window, looking down at him, wondering how she might help. And then an even more hurtful practice began. After dinner almost every night, Harry began to excuse himself, leaving Stacey downstairs to help with the dishes. He went up to Lisette's suite—and closed the door behind him.

In the face of all this, Stacey stubbornly kept her nose in her books, practised her flying, did the thousand things that the mistress of a house was supposed to do—and worried. May the tenth would mark the day when Harry and Lisette had complied with his grandmother's Will. And then what? she agonised. Then once again he won't need a wife, and would turn me out to pasture? Would they sell Rosedale? If they did, what would happen to the Fallons? The thought became so strong that, towards the end of April, two days after she had passed all her flight tests and examinations, she went down to the kitchen and asked.

'You mean you're worried about us?' Millie was up to her elbows in dough, and four pie tins were scattered across her work table. 'Apple pies—can you imagine that? Springtime, and we have fresh apples for pies! Don't ask me where they come from.' She stopped long enough to smile over the tops of her bifocals, which had slipped down to the end of her nose.

'That's all taken care of, you know. Harry didn't tell you?'

Stacey grimaced. One more item to add to the ten thousand that Harry didn't get around to telling her. 'No, I suppose it slipped his mind,' she said. 'Tell me about it.' She walked over to the always-filled coffee pot and helped herself to a mug.

'Why, it ain't no big thing,' chuckled Millie. 'The

contractor over to your ranch has finished with expanding the house. When they decide—Harry and Lisette, that is—whatever they're going to do with Rosedale here, me and Frank, we're packing up and moving over to Rancho Miraflores.'

'To—to Miraflores? Expanding the house?' Stacey was stunned, and her face showed it.

'You don't want us to come?' Millie asked anxiously.

'Don't want—of course I want you to come,' Stacey returned. 'It just was so startling that—it—overwhelmed me, that's all. Of course I want you to come—both of you—and the new girl too, if she wants to. Wonderful!' She skipped around the table and traded a bear hug for a kiss and a covering of flour.

'Now you just get out of here,' Millie warned, 'or the pies won't be ready for supper, and you know what the mister will say about that!'

Stacey obeyed with alacrity. She needed to think about this. 'The mister' was set on improving her property at the expense of his own, it seemed. Or was he expecting to leave Millie and Frank at Miraflores while he looked for a new place of his own, then move out after the pretend-marriage was finished? She felt bewildered, but one thing was sure—she owed the man some favours. He could send his entire staff to Rancho Miraflores if he wanted!

But no sooner was she out of the kitchen than she found herself trapped by Lisette. 'I've been meaning to have a talk with you,' the older woman said. She was purring, as if the world was finally revolving in her direction. 'Come into the living room for a minute.'

'That's a lovely little suit you've got on,' Stacey managed to get out.

'Sit down.' Lisette gestured towards the couch. 'Cigarette?'

'No. I don't smoke.' There was an uneasy moment of silence, while the older woman lit up, using her ivory holder.

'You don't have many vices, do you?' There was something in her voice that jarred Stacey's teeth, some sort of predatory warning, as if a jungle cat were prowling.

'I—I guess I have as many as most,' she answered. 'Except smoking.'

'Stealing other people's men seems high on your list!'

'What? You mean Harry?' The other woman was pacing up and down in front of her, and Stacey felt the disadvantage of being seated.

'Yes, I mean Harry. Who else in the world is there?'

'You make it sound as if I came along and picked him up from where you left him. You don't know Harry as well as you think you do if that's what you had in mind.'

'I know Harry a lot better than you'll ever know him, you stupid little bitch. I grew up with Harry. Surely you don't believe we lived together in this house for so long without anything happening?'

'Anything? I don't understand.'

'Of all the—heaven protect me from the innocent! I'm talking about Harry and me. We were lovers for years, right under dear old Grandma's nose. And still would be, if it weren't for you, damn you! What happened? Did he give you a fling and get you pregnant?'

'Why—why—' Stacey's anger came up and overflowed. 'I don't know what you think you're up to,' she snarled, 'but I don't believe a word of it. Harry's too—too honest to do something like that. I don't believe it. If it were so, how come you didn't marry him a long time ago, when you had the chance?'

'So I made a mistake.' Lisette tipped her ash off on to the rug. 'I actually thought Burnet had more money. And he turned out to be as big a four-flusher as Harry. You don't really know why Harry married you, do you?'

'Of course I do,' said Stacey indignantly. 'We fell in love. He needed me, and I needed him! And I wasn't pregnant—at that time. And I think that's all you and I have to talk about, Mrs Burnet. Just keep away from me. If I really lose my temper you could get knocked on your—lovely foundation!'

'Well, I'm going to tell you anyway, you stupid bitch. Luckily the detectives I hired struck pay dirt on you. You're the sole owner of Rancho Miraflores, aren't you? All that lovely oil just waiting to be sucked up out of the ground.'

'So what?'

'So I don't suppose you read the financial pages, do you? Parsons Oil—isn't that the outfit that pays your royalties for the field? Don't bother to deny it, I know it's true.'

'Again—so what?'

'So Parsons Oil is in a great deal of trouble. Five dry holes they've drilled in the last six months. The outfit's on the ropes, believe me—the word is out all over Houston and Waco. So what does Harry do? He goes out of his way to play a little game with the poor little orphan girl, the owner of all that lovely oil. How about that?'

'What are you talking about?' The news was more than uncomfortable. Stacey had wondered for all those months. Why had Harry picked her up that first day at the airport? I'm not all *that* pretty, she told herself. And—and since then, he's been running everything. I gave him my power of attorney, and he's been running everything. How do I know how much oil he's been pumping out of my reserves? No, Harry wouldn't do that. How could he? Parsons Oil might do it, but not Harry! There were glinting tears in her wide eyes as she glared at Lisette. 'Get to the point. What are you talking about!'

'I'm talking about Harry.' The other woman could see how deeply her darts had penetrated, and was moving in for the *coup de grâce*. 'Why, you naïve little thing, you! You really don't know. Well, let me draw you a picture. Harry is Marsden Management. And what does he manage? Parsons Oil, of course.'

'And Westland Cattle?' The words came out in a whisper of apprehension.

'Yes, of course, Westland Cattle. And Federal Electronics too. Did you think he supported all his pretensions on a fly-by-night management corporation?'

Stacey struggled back to her feet and glared back at the little gadfly. That was what had been the difference in Lisette's appearance—the look of vengeance. It glared out of the sallow cheeks, the glittering eyes, the straight thin mouth.

'So he owns them all,' she sighed, wiping the tears away with her fingers. Her mind was racing. Harry. No matter what he owned, how he acted, what he did, she loved him. If he stripped her of all her property she would still love him. If every word Lisette had said was true, her love still would hold.

She patted the other woman sympathetically on the shoulder. 'And if he owns all that, and does all that, and thinks all that—I still love him,' she stated flatly. 'And there's nothing you can do to make me stop loving him. Save your breath.' She spun on her heel and walked out of the room, missing the contorted hatred that set Lisette's body trembling in a fit of desperate passion.

CHAPTER TEN

STACEY cornered him at the dinner table a few days later. 'Harry, would you tell me something?'

'I don't know. It depends on what it is.'

'It's only five more days before the will runs out. What are you going to do?'

'That's more than one question, and I don't have all the answers yet.'

'You could tell me about the things that *are* settled?'

'Okay.' He stopped long enough to munch on the steak. 'Now, first of all, there's Lisette. I guess you know that her so-called illness was a fake. Oh, she felt bad, and suffered from malnutrition, but the basic cause of it is alcoholism. I've argued and raved, but I can't convince her that she needs treatment. And that's the first step with alcoholics—they have to admit that they're sick. Lisette is not ready to admit it. She's sure she can give it up any time she pleases.'

'I know,' Stacey said hesitantly. 'Moving from Army post to Army post, you see them all. That's one of the leading causes of disability in the service—alcoholism. So that's what you've been doing with her every night?'

'That's it.' He set both knife and fork down on the plate and stared at her. She did her best to dodge behind the curtain of her hair. '*Is* that all, Stacey? Do I detect a little jealousy behind all these questions?'

'Me? Jealous? Why would I be jealous? I'm only the hired hand around here. And come to think of it, I'm not even sure what the wages are.'

'That's fancy footwork, too,' he admired. 'You can change the subject faster than any girl I've ever met!'

She stared at him. Surely he doesn't think I'll comment on that insult, does he? she thought. I may have

170

been born yesterday, but I've learned a great deal since then.

'You're talking to yourself,' Harry said mildly. 'Interesting subject?'

'What about Lisette?' she prodded, trying to change the subject again.

'Well, as you say, we're coming down to the wire, and there's no immediate solution in sight. But you understand, she's still my charge.'

'And?'

'And I have to discharge that responsibility before I can take on any new ones. You can see that?'

No, I can't, she shrieked inside. 'Yes,' her well-trained lips responded. Harry gave a sigh of contentment.

'That's one of the many things I like about you, Stacey. You understand things, and react sensibly.'

Sure I do, she told herself. I think I'll go jump in Lake Waco. They say that a non-swimmer like me could drown in four minutes. You bet I'm sensible. I wonder if I could hire a hit-man from the mob to get rid of that woman?

'Whatever the reason,' he continued, 'Lisette is too emotionally insecure to agree that we should sell the estate and split the proceeds. In the end I suspect I'll just have to resign my share and let her take it over, lock, stock and barrel.'

'Then on the tenth,' she said hesitantly, 'I suppose our need for play-acting will be over?' As soon as the words were out of her mouth she regretted them. I don't really want to know, she told herself fiercely. No matter what the answer is, I don't want to know. Please God, don't let him answer!

'Yes,' he said slowly, pushing his empty plate away, 'I suppose we should say that on the tenth our road show will close down, and we can get on with life. The tenth? There's something else about that date that sticks in the back of my mind.'

'It's my birthday,' she said flatly. 'I'll be nineteen on that date.'

'That's it—of course. Your birthday. And you'll be nineteen—a ripe old age. At least I won't feel so much like a cradle—I mean, at least you'll be almost out of your teens, won't you?'

The bitterness blocked her ears, sent tears to her eyes—and he had continued to talk.

'. . . so you can see you can't stay here after that,' he was saying. 'I think you'd best go back to Miraflores.'

'On the tenth?' she asked, trying to hold back the tears.

'Yes, on the tenth,' he said. 'Didn't I make that clear? When will your classes end for this semester?'

'On the fifteenth,' she offered sadly.

'Well then, let's say you leave here and go to the penthouse from the tenth until the fifteenth, and then back to Miraflores. Then in the fall, we can make—'

'I don't think we should plan that far ahead,' she said woodenly. 'In the fall I think I'll transfer to the University of Texas, at the Austin campus.' She forced herself to look straight ahead, trying to avoid his eyes. He got up from his chair slowly, reaching for the dirty dishes.

'Damn it, Stacey, you haven't been listening to a word I said,' he complained. 'I've got business to tend to. Why don't you go on to bed, and I'll look in before you fall asleep.'

She watched the muscles ripple under his silk shirt as he walked to the door. 'Yes, Daddy,' she muttered rebelliously.

When she awoke to the new day Harry was gone. 'There was an emergency call,' Millie explained as she piled a plate high with scrambled eggs and honey-cured ham. 'I didn't get the particulars—something about a fire. He took off in a cloud of goose-grease. Didn't you hear the helicopter?'

'If I did I must have turned over and gone back to

sleep,' sighed Stacey. 'How can anyone my age sleep so much?'

'There must be a million reasons,' Millie returned. 'I don't suppose you've been to the doctor lately?' Oh no, not that one again, Stacey sighed to herself. Not that one. I'm not pregnant, damnit! I'm not even—

'Can you keep a secret, Millie?' The housekeeper favoured her with a big smile, and leaned both elbows on the work counter, waiting for an important confidence.

'Of course I can,' she replied.

'So can I.' Stacey laughed as she cleaned her plate, grabbed for an apple, and headed for school.

The days marched slowly by, and Harry did not come. She haunted the office, looking for news. On the eighth of May Amie Moreland came back. Stacey haunted her until she managed to slip out of her coat, pat her hair, and order up a cup of coffee. As she leaned back in her executive chair she looked at Stacey again. 'You mean that rotten devil didn't even tell you where he was going?'

'Well, I was asleep,' Stacey started off lamely, then pulled herself up. Why should I defend him? That's exactly what he did, the rotten—'Yes, that's exactly what he did,' she grumbled. 'And then he hasn't called, or written, or—what is he up to, Amie?' And why do I sound as if I were begging for a handout? I only want to know where my husband is. Is that too much to ask? To know where my husband—

The strain was too much. Tears poured down her face like a spring gulley-washer. She was too weak to stand. She backed up slowly until a chair bumped against the back of her knees, and fell into it, making no attempt to mop up the mess.

'Hey now,' Amie comforted, 'No man on earth is worth that. Calm down. There's more to this than meets the eye. Have you seen a doctor lately?'

And that was the last straw. Broken, sobbing, bent over to protect against the pain in her stomach, Stacey spilled it all out. Everything, from the beginning, on that early flight from Dallas, to the day before yesterday. By the end of her story Amie Moreland was storming up and down the room, pounding one hand into the other.

'Why, that rotten—' she sputtered. 'You mean—just like that—he hired you to be his wife?'

'It really isn't that—well, at first I did it for him as a favour, because he had done me a favour, Amie. And then it—it just grew. I didn't know where to stop. I didn't *want* to stop, can't you see?'

'Oh, I can see all right. You feel head over heels in love with him. No?'

'I—yes. I couldn't help it, Amie. I didn't *want* to fall in love with him, honest!'

'Yes, I can see that, my dear. Here, use my handkerchief. It's a lot bigger than that piece of lace you're fooling with.' Amie bustled into the corner of the room and came back with two full shot glasses. 'Here, drink this, love. Down the hatch.'

'But—but I don't drink.'

'Me neither. Down the hatch.' They both tilted their glasses and emptied them. The liquor burned its way down Stacey's throat and hit her stomach like a major brush fire. She gasped and choked on it, unable to breathe. Amie was having her own similar problems.

'Now then.' The older woman cleared her throat and sat down behind the desk again. 'He's down in Galveston—well, not exactly there. There was a fire on Parsons Oil Rig Sixteen, out in the gulf. Naturally we called in trained fire-fighters. But your husband— damn—but Harry is never one to leave things alone. He had to be there. He's still out there on one of the fire ships. I can understand why he couldn't call or write. But he could have told me to call. Damn that man! Now, what are we going to do about you?'

'Nothing, I guess,' Stacey muttered, dabbing at her eyes. 'I feel better just telling somebody about it. It's all been building up inside me for months. I'm sure you have enough troubles of your own.'

'One thing you can be sure of is when he gets back, I'm going to give him a piece of my mind. You ought to, too.'

'I can't do that, Amie. I really can't.' A distant memory tickled her mind. 'My father always said, don't give people a piece of your mind, when you're liable to need it yourself!'

'I'll say one thing for you, Stacey, you've a strong character,' said Amie. 'If I'd been through all this I'd be having a nervous breakdown right about now. Anything you want me to do?'

'I don't think so. The day after tomorrow I'll be leaving the mansion. I'm almost finished with final exams now. I'll come in to the apartment for the remaining five days of school. And then I suppose I'll go back to the ranch, or something.'

'And brood about him, I suppose? You really love him, don't you?'

'I—I guess so. I don't know. I've never been in love before. Maybe it's only an infatuation?' Stacey sent an appealing look across the desk. Tell me that's what it is, her eyes pleaded. Tell me it will pass away soon. Tell me!

'I don't know what to tell you,' Amie sympathised. 'When I met Karl I knew he was my man right away. But my mother says when she first met my father she didn't even like him. He had to court her for a year before she discovered otherwise.'

'I just—I don't know what to say, Amie. Do you know when he'll be coming home?'

'No, I don't. It could be as early as tomorrow—or it could be as late as next week. The oil business is a funny thing.'

'I have to run, Amie,' said Stacey. 'I have another class, and it's all the way across the campus.'

'All right, love. Study hard, and don't worry. Basically, Harry is really a fine man.'

The next day, her last at Rosedale, was a Thursday, and Stacey had no classes to account for. She spent an hour in the kitchen helping Millie Fallon, then drove her Eagle down to the airport for another lesson. This time it was a fixed wing solo, in a Cessna Commander. She junketed in a great circle around Waco, sweeping almost a hundred miles in each direction before she came back in, shot several practice landings, and made her way back to the house.

Millie had left her a note on the kitchen table. 'Frank and I have gone to Temple. One of our nephews has had an accident. Supper in refrigerator.' She poked around in the big cooler and made herself a ham and chicken sandwich. Nothing else interested her. She washed it down with a glass of milk, then went slowly up the stairs. There was packing to do.

She went about it lackadasically, cramming her college clothes into the lightweight flight bag, and saving her big suitcase for the formal wear, the accumulation of her months of living in the big house. Don't leave anything behind, her mind niggled at her. Take everything. You may never come back this way again. The thought was not exactly comforting, and when the sound of a helicopter filled the twilight, and landing lights stabbed down, her first thought was that Harry had finally come home. 'Be practical,' she told herself. 'He's seen you for months in blouse and jeans. Get dressed! Get gussied up!'

Her uncertain hand reached into the bag she had been packing and extracted a lightweight A-line shift in pastel yellow. It fitted her mood, and highlighted her hair, so she dived into it, all the while telling herself to 'Hurry, hurry!' The sound of the motor could still be heard, the blades idling, and sending out their familiar 'whap—whap—whap' as they rotated slowly. She ran a brush through her hair and, not bothering with make-up, ran for the stairs and out into the dark behind the house.

Her eyes were not adjusted to the dark, but she could

see the blurred figure of a tall man moving up from the paddock. This is no time to hang back, she yelled to herself. Go for broke! She ran across the uneven ground towards him, until her right foot slipped on a small rock and she pitched forward into his arms.

'Oh, Harry,' she laughed,' I've missed you so much!'

'Have you really?' said the gruff voice above her head.

'You're not—oh, my God! George. George Delano! What are you doing here?'

'Why, I've come to get you, little Stacey. We're going to be married!'

'Let me go!' She struggled in his grip but could not break free. 'You must be some sort of idiot,' she snapped at him. 'I'm already married. Let me go! How in the world did you know I was here?'

'Would you believe it,' he laughed, 'your house-guest told me. And offered me a bundle to carry you off. Married, are you? Then we'll have to write this off as a kidnapping. And when—or if—your husband gets you back, maybe he won't want you.'

'Why are you doing this?' she screamed at him as he urged her up to the house and into the hall.

'For money, of course. One way or another, for money.'

'You're a fool, George. If I scream there'll be people around here like crazy. Then what? Let me go!'

'In just a minute. Go ahead and scream. See how many people there are to help you! It took long enough to arrange for them all to be away, baby!' In the light of the hallway she looked up at him, and did not like what she saw. His face was contorted, his eyes were bright with determination, and she remembered. George, the one who liked to hurt people.

'Hold her still, for heaven's sakes!' The voice was behind her, a woman's cracked soprano.

'Lisette—get help! He's a madman or something!' shrieked Stacey.

'I wouldn't be surprised. But you were engaged to him, weren't you?' The laughter startled Stacey.

'Lisette? Not you! You wouldn't—I'm leaving tomorrow. What harm can I do to you?'

'None at all,' the older woman laughed. 'Not now. Hold her still. Get her mouth pried open.' George had her in a firm grip, one she could not fight off. One of his hands came around and pulled at her nose, forcing her mouth open.

'There's the little dear,' laughed Lisette. She tugged at the cap of a bottle she held in both hands, and Stacey could smell the overwhelming odour of alcohol as she came closer. 'You're not leaving tomorrow, girl. You're leaving tonight. And after I tell Harry that you ran away with your boy-friend, that ought to be the end of you. Hold her still!'

She shook two pills out of the bottle and forced them between Stacey's lips. 'Swallow nicely, child,' she laughed. 'It's the pill you're used to.' George tilted her head back, and it was either swallow or choke. Stacey swallowed.

'A couple more,' muttered Lisette. Unable to control her own actions, Stacey's fears grew to be more than she could handle. Her struggles ceased, and she fell limp in his arms. Unable to fight back, she swallowed three more pills that the other woman crammed in her mouth.

'That ought to be enough,' Lisette said. 'Now get her out to the helicopter. Where are you taking her.'

'I know a place,' growled George. 'An abandoned spread out by Sweetwater. And the less I tell you, the better off we'll both be. I am to have a little fun out of this.' He swung Stacey up and threw her over his shoulder in a fireman's carry, and went back to the machine. The pilot waited for them, a puzzled look on his face.

'Give me a hand here,' George demanded, and between them they slid her into the middle of the bench seat. She was beginning to regain her courage, and the pills had not yet taken effect. The pilot climbed in beside her and revved up the engine. She managed to get both hands on his arm, and he looked over at her. 'They're kidnapping me!' she shouted at the top of her voice.

The startled pilot looked over at George. 'Kidnapping? I thought you said she was sick. I'm not flying any kidnapping route, buddy.'

'The hell you aren't,' George returned. 'Take a look at this, fellow.' He displayed an old-fashioned Colt .45 Peacemaker, its long barrel wavering between Stacey and the pilot.

'I'm not flying you anywhere,' the pilot insisted.

'So try this!' George screamed at him. The heavy weapon rose, and the barrel smashed down on the pilot's head. He slumped over immediately, losing his grip on the controls. George kicked him out of the aircraft with one foot, then forced Stacey into the left-hand seat. 'You!' He gestured with the gun. 'You can fly this thing. I've watched you for a month.'

'Me?' she returned in surprise. The pills were gradually working. 'You want me to drive to my own funeral?'

'Just get it up in the air, or you're a dead chick.' He waved the muzzle of the gun under her nose. Up? It was beginning to sound like a logical thing to do. Her ears were buzzing, and nothing seemed important any more. She yanked back on the pitch control and gunned the engine. The helicopter vaulted straight up, snarling to a thousand feet. The sound of waltz music buzzed in her head. She swung the controls right and left to the cadenza of the dance, and the chopper swayed as directed.

'You're turning green, George,' she sighed, hating to have the music disrupted. 'That's a silly gun. It ought to be in a museum. Does it still shoot?'

'You'll find out if there's any funny business. Go west!'

'West?' She peered at the compass. Her eyes were

blurred, and she could barely read the meter. A voice blared at her from the loudspeaker over her head.

'Helicopter K610, you are making an unauthorised crossing of the landing pattern. This is Waco tower. Return to five hundred feet.'

Stacey nodded. It certainly was the right sort of order to give. Her hands moved, and the bottom fell out of the world as the machine dropped like a stone to the lower altitude. George, she noted, was still green, and hanging on to a strap by the door. He looked as if he was going to—and he did.

'Helicopter K610.' It was the same voice. 'Are you in some trouble?'

She fumbled for the microphone switch. 'No, thank you,' she carolled gaily, 'except he's kidnapping me!'

George growled and pulled the microphone wires loose. He raised his hand to hit her, and raised the contents of his stomach at the same time. 'Go to Sweetwater,' he said hoarsely.

Go to Sweetwater—what a lovely name. Why not? But her eyes could not focus on the map he was waving at her. She smiled gaily at him, and the waltz music surrounded her again. Back and forth the ship swayed as she danced it across the sky in three-quarter time. Sweetwater, I really ought to land. But I could make a horrible mess of it. The fuel tanks have to be empty, right? George was back upright again. He jabbed at her breast with the long barrel of the gun. His gun hand shook, while the other covered his mouth.

'That hurts,' she complained in a little-girl voice. The pills were really taking over. Obviously it was a game they were playing, and all she had to do was to fool George. Hide and seek? The first one home wins? Gleefully she blinked her blurry eyes at the compass, set a north-westerly heading, and began a great circle that took her over Hamilton, Stephenville, Clerbourne, and Waxahachie, with one eye on the fuel consumption gauge, and the other on the highways below, which was serving as her real navigational guide. Another pithy remark from her father: 'When you really get lost, just follow the railroad or the highway!' Seat-of-the-pants flying. She swept the machine back into three-quarter time, and giggled as George lost control of his stomach again.

'Are you sure we're headed for Sweetwater?' her nervous passenger asked.

'Of course we are, George,' she kept repeating. 'Why not?'

'How much longer?' he mumbled desperately.

'Not too long,' she said in that high little-girl voice. She squinted at the gauge. It was easier to see with just one eye. The needle was bouncing off the bottom peg. The tanks were almost empty, and out of her side window she could see the markers. They were back exactly where they had started.

'George,' she said, 'I think we have to land here.'

'God, I don't care,' he groaned. 'Land the damn thing before I jump.'

'Oh, poor George,' she sympathised, deep in the clutches of the pills. 'I don't think you'll be a very successful kidnapper, George.' And at that moment the motor sputtered, spurted again, and completely stopped. In the instant silence that followed Stacey shifted the blades into the auto-giro position. 'You'd better hang on, George,' she carolled happily to him. 'I can't seem to see the ground, and we might hit something.'

But George won't be mad, she told herself. He's very forgiving. She was unable to tell how right she was. When the motor had stopped, George had fainted. And now the helicopter was swinging, lacking motor drive on the stabilising tail rotor. It swung around, slammed into the side of the barn at Rosedale, and the entire fragile aircraft collapsed around her ears.

So she missed all the rest of it. Everything went happily black. She missed the noise, the confusion, the sudden appearance of that angry man, the fire—everything. Even the eventual explosion that spread remnants of the aircraft over a two-hundred-yard circle, and burned the empty barn completely down to the ground.

CHAPTER ELEVEN

'WELL,' the soft voice said in her ear, 'you've decided to come around, have you?'

'I—I guess so,' she returned muzzily. 'I—' She was about to utter that old bromide, 'Where am I?' when she suddenly knew. She was in her bed, at Rosedale. She struggled mightily to get up, but her arms were slow to respond. 'I have to be out of here today,' she muttered. 'Oh, Millie, today is the tenth, and I've got to go. He said so.'

'Nonsense,' the housekeeper said gently. 'Today's the twelfth, and you don't have to go anyplace. How do you feel?'

'I feel fine—except—why am I so sleepy?'

'Five Valium pills will do that,' the housekeeper said cheerfully.

'You said the twelfth? What—lord, I've got a final exam today a nine o'clock! I have to go, or waste the whole quarter's work.'

'You're as bad a patient as he is,' chuckled Millie. 'Amie Moreland took care of all that. The University has granted you an exemption from the rest of your exams.'

'As he is?' The gleam had gone from Stacey's lovely eyes. 'Harry was hurt?'

'More mad than hurt, love. He came home unexpectedly, not more than twenty minutes after you'd left. You should have heard him give Her Majesty the business—her with that cock and bull story about you running away with the Delano fellow. So he sat there by the telephone and got all the radar stations in the heart of Texas looking for you. Especially after Waco Tower reported that you were being kidnapped. Did you know that the Army had two helicopters trailing you all the way? Harry is a Colonel in the reserve, you know.'

Of course he is, Stacey told herself. 'Oh, how nice. How wonderfully nice.' And it was. Somebody cared. Somebody important cared! 'But he was hurt?'

'Hey, when you were hovering over the house all that time he was out in the paddock waiting. Boy, was he charged up! "She'll set it down exactly right", he kept saying—but then you missed, didn't you?'

'It was those pills,' she protested. 'I couldn't get my eyes focused Do you think they'll pull my licence?'

'Don't be a fool, Stacey. You're a heroine,' Millie assured her. 'Well, anyway, you crashed, and he was in there after you like a streak of lightning. You had a little bump on your forehead, and now you've got a dandy black eye.'

'And that's when he got hurt? Carrying me out of the chopper?'

'No, not exactly. He brought you up the hill and left you with us, then he went back for Delano.'

'And that's how he got hurt?'

'No, not exactly. "Smartest little girl in all the world," he said when he came back with Delano. "Ran it till the tanks were empty, shut off all the switches, but there's a gasoline vapour in the tanks. It's bound to blow".'

'And that's when he got hurt?' Stacey sat up, cramming her hands into her mouth.

'No, not exactly. Wait—you'll laugh.'

I'll laugh, she thought. I love him and I'll laugh. He went into the helicopter to get me, knowing it was about to blow up, and I'll laugh! 'What happened?' she screamed. 'Tell me what happened!'

'OK, OK,' the housekeeper laughed. 'But don't yell—he's in the next room, sleeping. Well, anyway, he had us all duck down, and sure enough the machine blew up. Like ten thousand Fourth of July celebrations, it was. Skyrockets, firecrackers—oh, my! And then the barn caught fire. All of us, there was nothing to do, so we just sat there and watched. But not your husband. He was raving mad—not about the chopper, or the fire, but because Delano made a nasty remark about you. He pulled that guy up by his shirt tails and almost beat him to death, he did. And broke his hand doing it. That's probably the only reason why he stopped. Now, you get on the outside of this breakfast, and get some more sleep. Y'hear?'

'Oh, I hear all right.' But sleep I don't need, Stacey told herself. She tossed down the orange juice, sipped at the hot coffee, and took one bite out of the toast. It was difficult getting up, but the more she moved the better she moved. The girl who looked at her out of the full-length mirror on the bathroom door was a stranger to her. Snarled blonde hair tumbled down where it would around a thin stretched face. Wide trembling eyes, one of them underscored by a discoloured swollen lump. Shaky lips, trying valiantly to be still. Someone had poured her into a see-through nightgown, a little lacy thing that she would never have had the nerve to wear. Oh well, she sighed, what you see is what you get. I owe him—for everything. For saving me from the Delanos, for spurring me into a new life, and most of all, for believing in me instead of Lisette. And then he saved my life. I owe him, and I've only got one thing to give to a man who already has everything: me. And then I'll leave.

Her body responded beautifully as her feet carried her through the connecting door and into his bedroom. His room was not a match for hers. Small, utilitarian, heavy furniture, and a bed almost as big as the waterbed at the Penthouse. He was lying flat on his back under a single white sheet, his right hand resting on top of the sheet and encased in a small plaster cast. Stacey went around the bed, stopped to slip out of her nightgown, and crawled in beside him.

The heat of his body was like an oven. She snuggled up against him, using one finger to push back the unruly lock of hair at his forehead. We just fit, she told herself hysterically. With my toes on his, the top of my head just fits under his chin. I didn't realise that the hair on his chest was so wiry. And does he ever need a shave! It was her wandering hands that were conveying the information to her mind.

Harry stirred, still not quite awake. 'Stacey,' he muttered. 'I love you.' Her heart stopped. I love you? Can the subconscious lie? Probably! What do I do next?

She snuggled closer, nibbling at the tip of his ear. He growled in his sleep, and moved an inch or two. Without quite knowing what she was up to, she came up on one elbow and teased the tips of her ripe breasts across the taut skin of his chest. He stirred, squirmed, and opened one startled eye.

'What the hell are you doing?' he rasped. The gruffness of his voice forced her back from him.

'I—I'm seducing you,' she half-whispered.

The glare turned into a smile. 'Well, you're not doing a very good job of it,' he chuckled.

'I'm doing the best I know how,' she returned petulantly. 'I've never seduced a man before. You could help. I love you.'

'I wouldn't be much help to you,' he grinned. 'I've never seduced a man before myself. And I love you too, Stacey.'

'You—you do? For a long time?' The hopeful note overflowed her voice and lit up the room.

Harry struggled to control the laughter, but was not too successful. 'Not exactly,' he said. 'I was going to say since Amie read me the riot act a few days ago. Lord, that woman has got a mean tongue! But truthfully, I fell in love with you when I saw your sensitive loving heart, dealing with my grandmother. I was afraid that with you it was just a teenage infatuation. Until Amie told me, at great length, how wrong I was. What the devil are you doing now?'

'I read in a book once that if you did this—' Stacey grabbed his good hand and pressed it against her breast. 'Aren't you—aren't you going to teach me what to do next?'

'You're darn right I am,' he returned, 'but not until the day after tomorrow.'

'I—I don't understand.' She could feel the whole weight of rejection fall on her shoulders. 'Why not tomorrow? Why not today? Is it because of my oil wells? Are you really trying to steal my oil? That's what Lisette said—that you were trying to steal my oil to keep your company from going bust.'

'Nobody can be as naïve as you are,' he chuckled. 'Of course I'm not trying to steal your oil wells. I'm a big-time thief, not a penny-ante one. I'm trying to steal you!'

She no longer had to hold his hand at her breast; it was doing well enough on its own. And causing a wild war to rage among her senses. A wild unquenchable thirst ravaged her mind, ran rampant over all the Lutheran truths of her upbringing, and smashed square into the wall of her practical curiosity.

'And you're not bound to Lisette any more?'

'After what she did to you? Nonsense! I turned her over to the Sheriff, along with that Delano fool. Did you know she hired a gaggle of detectives to find him? They deserve each other. Next question?'

'And me. Do you still think I'm infatuated with you—that I'm still a kid?'

'Holy Hannah, what a question at a time like this!' His hand was forming and shaping her breast, teasing the bronze tip. 'No, I don't think you're a kid, nor do I think you're suffering through an infatuation. My God, this cast makes me clumsy!'

'Well—then—' she stammered, following her own logic to its end, 'why do I have to wait until the day after tomorrow?'

'Because that's when we're getting married, you little

nut. We're going to take a helicopter, and you're going to fly us as far away from here as we can get, and find us a Justice of the Peace who will perform a very quiet wedding. Two weddings for us would be a mite suspicious, you know. And then after that, I'll teach you all about seduction.'

'But that's what I don't understand. I thought we were already married. I've thought so for months. And so have the Fallons. And everybody in the neighbourhood.' As she talked her hands were roaming again, up and down his rib-cage, across his stomach, down his heavily muscled thighs.

'And everybody at the Corporation knows it,' she continued grimly, 'and almost everybody at the University, and everybody at Rancho Miraflores, and—'

'In fact, I'm the only one who doesn't know, is that what you're saying?' Harry's face was losing its stiffness, his breath becoming sharper. His good hand reached for her shoulder and pulled her forward, flat against him. 'Lord, how I want you, girl.'

She could feel the tension spread throughout his long lean body, and wild horses rode rampant through her being. 'Let this be the time, Lord,' she whispered.

'What did you say?'

'I said, why are you so stubborn? Why are you the only one in McClennan County who doesn't believe we're already married?'

He buried his face in the warmth of her hair, nibbled at her ear, then pushed her away so his tongue could touch madly at the tip of her aroused breast.

'I'm beginning to recall the details of the ceremony,' he laughed as he pulled her close again. 'You were wearing an ivory dress, because you were two days too late for white, and your teacher at the School of Seduction had just given you a passing grade in his course. Right?'

'Oh, I still wore the white dress,' Stacey answered

dreamily. 'I understand that a lot of girls lie about that these days.' She laughed and waited, trembling, expectantly, as he began the first lesson.

What the press says about Harlequin romance fiction...

"When it comes to romantic novels...
Harlequin is the indisputable king."
— *New York Times*

"...always with an upbeat, happy ending."
— *San Francisco Chronicle*

"Women have come to trust these
stories about contemporary people,
set in exciting foreign places."
— *Best Sellers*, New York

"The most popular reading matter of
American women today."
— *Detroit News*

"...a work of art."
— *Globe & Mail*, Toronto